STRANGER THINGS IN HEAVEN
AND EARTH ...

Wexford drank white wine, very dry and as cold as the Olive and Dove was able to produce it which, tonight, was around blood heat. He began the evening by congratulating his friend Dr. Crocker on the accuracy of his on-the-spot estimate of the time of death. The post-mortem had put the murder at between seven and nine-thirty.

"Eight-thirty's the most probable," he said, "on her way from the bus stop." He sipped his warm wine. "She was a strong healthy woman—until someone put a knife in her. One stab wound pierced a lung and the other the left ventricle. No signs of disease, no abnormalties. Except one. I think in these days you could call it abnormality."

"What d'you mean?" said Crocker.

"She was a virgin," Wexford replied.

A
Sleeping Life

RUTH RENDELL

BANTAM BOOKS
TORONTO · NEW YORK · LONDON · SYDNEY · AUCKLAND

All of the characters in this book are fictitious, and any resemblance to actual persons, living or dead, is purely coincidental.

A SLEEPING LIFE

*A Bantam Book / published by arrangement with
Doubleday & Company Inc.*

PRINTING HISTORY

*Doubleday edition published October 1978
2nd printing ... October 1978*

Mystery Guild edition November 1978

*Bantam edition / February 1980
2nd printing ... May 1980
3rd printing ... June 1986*

Bantam Books are published by Bantam Books, Inc. Its trademark, consisting of the words "Bantam Books" and the portrayal of a rooster, is Registered in U.S. Patent and Trademark Office and in other countries. Marca Registrada. Bantam Books, Inc., 666 Fifth Avenue, New York, New York 10103.

*For Elaine and Leslie Gray,
with affection and gratitude.*

Those have most power to hurt us, that we love;
We lay our sleeping lives within their arms.
O, thou hast raised up mischief to his height,
And found one to outname thy other faults.

Beaumont and Fletcher, *The Maid's Tragedy.*

1

Home early for once. Maybe he'd start getting home early regularly now August had begun, the silly season. Criminals as well as the law-abiding take their holidays in August. As he turned the car into his own road, Wexford remembered his grandsons would be there. Good. It would be light for another three hours, and he'd take Robin and Ben down to the river. Robin was always on about the river because his mother had read *The Wind in the Willows* to him, and his great desire was to see a water rat swimming.

Sylvia's car was parked outside the house. Odd, thought Wexford. He'd understood Dora was having the boys for the afternoon as well as the evening and that they'd be staying the night. As he edged his own car past his daughter's into the drive, she came running out of the house with a screaming Ben in her arms and six-year-old Robin looking truculent at her heels. Robin rushed up to his grandfather.

"You promised we could see the water rat!"

"So you can as far as I'm concerned and if there's one about. I thought you were staying the night."

Sylvia's face was crimson, with rage or perhaps just from haste. It was very hot.

"Well, they're not. Thanks to my dear husband, nobody's going anywhere even though it does happen to be our wedding anniversary. Will you shut up, Ben! He's bringing a client home for dinner instead, if you please, and I, of course, as usual have to be the one to do the cooking and fetch the kids."

"Leave them here," said Wexford. "Why not?"

"Yes, leave us here," Robin shouted. *"Go on."*

"Oh, no, that's out of the question. Why do you have to encourage them, Dad? I'm taking them home and Neil can have the pleasure of putting them to bed for once."

She thrust both children into the car and drove off. The windows of the car were all open, and the yells of the two little boys, for Robin had begun to back his brother up, vied with the roar of the ill-treated engine. Wexford shrugged and went indoors. Some sort of scene had evidently been taking place, but he knew his wife better than to suppose she would be much disturbed by it. True to his expectations, she was sitting placidly in the living room watching the tail end of a children's programme on television. A great many books had been pulled out of the shelves, and on a tower block of them sat a Teddy bear.

"What's got into Sylvia?"

"Women's Lib," said Dora Wexford. "If Neil wants to bring a client home he ought to cook the meal. He ought to come home in the afternoon and clean the house and lay the table. She's taken the children home for the sole purpose of getting him to put them to bed. And she's taking care to stir them up on the way to make sure he has a hard time of it."

"God. I always thought she was quite a sensible girl."

"She's got a bee in her bonnet about it. It's been going on for months. You are the people, we are the others. You are the masters, we are the chattels."

"Why haven't you told me about any of this?"

Dora switched off the television. "You've been busy. You wouldn't have wanted to listen to all this nonsense when you got home. I've been getting it every day."

Wexford raised his eyebrows. "It's nonsense?"

"Well, not entirely, of course. Men still do have a better time of it in this world than women, it's still a man's world. I can understand she doesn't like being stuck at home with the boys, wasting her life, as she puts it, while Neil gets more and more successful in his career." Dora smiled. "And she says she got more A Levels than he did. I can understand she gets bored when people come and the men talk to Neil about architecture and the women talk to her about polishing the bedroom furniture. Oh, I can *understand* it."

Her husband looked hard at her. "You feel that way too?"

"Never you mind," said Dora, laughing now. "Let's forget our rather tiresome child. You're so early we might go out somewhere after we've eaten. Would you like to?"

"Love to." He hesitated, said quickly, "It's not threatening their marriage, is it? I've always thought of them as being so happy together."

"We have to hope it'll pass. Anything we do or say would only make things worse, wouldn't it?"

"Of course. Now where shall we go? Cinema? Or how about the open-air theatre at Sewingbury?"

Before she could give him an answer, the phone rang.

"Sylvia," she said. "She's realised Ben left his Teddy. You get it, darling. Oh, and Reg . . . ? Would you say we'll drop it on our way? I can't stand another session of the wounded wives tonight."

Wexford lifted the receiver. It wasn't his daughter. Dora knew it wasn't even before he spoke. She knew that look. All he said was "Yes" and "Sure, I will," but she knew. He hung up and said, "They don't all go on holiday in August. A body in a field not half a mile from here."

"Is it . . . ?"

"Not one of the people," said her husband dryly. "One of the others." He tightened the tie he had loosened, rolled down his shirtsleeves. "I'll have to go straightway. What'll you do? Stir up the telly so I have a hard time of it putting it to rights? You must regret marrying me."

"No, but I'm working on it."

Wexford laughed, kissed her and drove back the way he had come.

Kingsmarkham is a sizeable town somewhere in the middle of Sussex, much built-up now on the Stowerton and Sewingbury sides, though open unspoilt country still remains at its northern end. There the High Street becomes the Pomfret Road, and there the pinewoods of Cheriton Forest clothe the hills.

Forest Road is the last street in the area to bear the postal address Kingsmarkham. It debouches directly from the Pomfret Road, but to reach it most of its few residents take the short cut from the end of the High Street by footpath across a field. Wexford parked his car at the point in Forest Road where this footpath entered it as an alley near the boundary fence of a pair of houses called Carlyle Villas. He swung into the alley and followed the footpath along a high privet hedge that bounded allotments. About a hundred yards ahead of him he could see a group of men gathered at the edge of a little copse.

Inspector Michael Burden was among them and so was Dr. Crocker, the police doctor, and a couple of photographers. As Wexford approached, Burden came up to him and said something in a low voice. Wexford nodded. Without looking at the body, he went up to Constable Loring who stood a little apart with a young man who looked pale and shaken.

"Mr. Parker?"

"That's right."

"I understand you found the body?"

Parker nodded. "Well, my son did."

He couldn't have been more than twenty-five himself.

"A *child?*" said Wexford.

"He doesn't realise. I hope not. He's only six."

They sat down on a wooden seat the council had put there for pensioners to rest on. "Tell me what happened."

"I'd taken him round to my sister's, give the wife a bit of a break while she was putting the other two to bed. I live in one of the bungalows in Forest Road, Bella Vista, the one with the green roof. We were coming back, along the path here, and Nicky was playing with a ball. It went in the long grass under the hedge and he went to look for it. He said, 'Dad, there's a lady down there.' I sort of knew, I don't know how. I went and looked and I—well, I know I shouldn't have, but I sort of pulled her coat over her chest. Nicky, you see, he's only six, and there was—well, blood, a mess."

"I do see," said Wexford. "You didn't move anything else?"

Parker shook his head. "I told Nicky the lady was ill and we'd go home and phone the doctor. I said she'd be all right. I don't think he realised. I hope not. I got him home and phoned your people. Honestly, I wouldn't have touched her if I'd been on my own."

"This was an exception, Mr. Parker." Wexford smiled at him. "I'd have done the same in your place."

"He won't have to . . . ? I mean, there'll be an inquest, won't there? I mean, I'll have to go, I know that, but . . ."

"No, no. Good God, no. Get off home now and we'll see you again later. Thanks for your help."

Parker got up off the seat, glanced at the photographers, the huddle round the body, then turned round. "It's not for me to . . . well, I mean, I do know who she is. Perhaps you don't . . ."

"No, we don't yet. Who is she?"

"Well, a Miss Comfrey. She didn't actually live here, her dad lives here." Parker pointed back down the path. "Carlyle Villas, the one with the blue paint. She must have been stopping there. Her dad's in hospital. He's an old man, he broke his hip, and she must have come down to see him."

"Thanks, Mr. Parker."

Wexford crossed the sandy path, and Burden stepped aside for him to look down at the body. It was that of a middle-aged woman, biggish and gaunt. The face was coated with heavy make-up, clotted scarlet on the mouth, streaky blue on the crepe eyelids, a ghastly ochreish layer on the planes of cheek and forehead. The grey eyes were wide and staring, and in them Wexford thought he saw—it must be his imagination—a sardonic gleam, a glare, even in death, of scorn.

A fringe of dark hair just showed under a tightly tied blue headscarf. The body was clothed in a blue-and-pink printed dress of some synthetic material, and the matching jacket, which had no fastenings, had been drawn across the bodice. One of the high-heeled shoes had come off and hung suspended on a tangle of brambles. Across the hips lay a large scarlet handbag. There were no rings on the hands, no watch on either wrist, but a heavy necklace of red glass beads round the neck, and the nails, though short, were painted the same scarlet.

He knelt down and opened the handbag, covering his fingers with his handkerchief. Inside was a key ring with three keys on it, a box of matches, a packet of king-size cigarettes from which four had been smoked, a lipstick, an old-fashioned powder compact, a wallet, in the bottom of the bag some loose change. No purse. No letters or documents. The wallet, which was an expensive new one of black leather, contained forty-two pounds. She hadn't been killed for the money she had on her.

There was nothing to give him a clue to her address, her occupation or even her identity. No credit card, no bank card, no cheque book.

He closed the bag and parted her jacket. The bodice of the dress was black with clotted blood, but plainly discernible in the dark matted mass were two cuts, the outward evidence of stab wounds.

2

Wexford moved away, and the doctor came back and knelt where he had knelt. He said to Loring,

"No sign of the weapon, I dare say?"

"No, sir, but we haven't made much of a search yet."

"Well, get searching, you and Gates and Marwood. A knife of some sort." The chances of its being there, he thought pessimistically, were slight. "And when you haven't found it," he said, "you can do a house-to-house down Forest Road. Get all you can about her and her movements, but leave Parker and Carlyle Villas to me and Mr. Burden."

Back to Dr. Crocker.

"How long has she been dead, Len?"

"Now, for God's sake, don't expect too much precision at this stage. Rigor's fully established, but the weather's been very hot, so its onset will have been more rapid. I'd say at least eighteen hours. Could be more."

"O.K." Wexford jerked his head at Burden. "There's nothing more here for us, Mike. Carlyle Villas and Parker next, I think."

Michael Burden was properly of too high a rank to accompany a chief inspector on calls of enquiry. He did so because that was the way they worked, the way it worked. They had always done so, and always would, in spite of disapproving mutterings from the Chief Constable.

Two tall men. Nearly twenty years separated them, and once they had been so dissimilar in appearance as to provide that juxtaposition of incongruities which is

7

the stuff of humour. But Wexford had lost his abundant fat and become almost a gaunt man, while Burden had always been lean. He was the better looking of the two by far, with classical features that would have been handsome had they been less pinched by sour experience. Wexford was an ugly man, but his was the face that arrested the eye, compelled even the eyes of women, because it had in it so much lively intelligence and zest for life, so much vigour, and in spite of his seniority, so much more of the essence of youth.

Side by side, they walked along the footpath and down the alley into Forest Road, not speaking, for there was nothing yet to say. The woman was dead, but death by murder is in a way not an end but a beginning. The lives of the naturally dead may be buried with them. Hers would now gradually be exposed, event after event, obscure though she had been, until it took on the character of a celebrity's biography.

From the alley, they turned to the right and stood outside the pair of houses, cottages really, in front of which Wexford had parked his car. The houses shared a single gable, and in its apex was a plaster plaque bearing their name and the date of their construction: Carlyle Villas, 1902. Wexford knocked at the blue front door with little hope of getting an answer. There was none, and no one came when they rang the bell on the neighbouring front door, a far more trendy and ambitious affair of wrought iron and reeded glass.

Frustrated at this most promising port of call, they crossed the street. Forest Road was a cul-de-sac, ending in a stone wall, behind which meadows swelled and the forest sprawled. It contained about a dozen houses, apart from Carlyle Villas, a clutch of tiny cottages at the wall end, two or three newer bungalows, a squat grey stone lodge that had once stood at the gates of a long-vanished mansion. One of the bungalows, built at the period when Hollywood's influence penetrated even this corner of Sussex, had windows of curved glass and a roof of green pantiles. Bella Vista.

The child Nicky was still up, sitting with his mother in a living room that had the same sort of untidy look as the one Wexford had left an hour before. But if Parker hadn't introduced this girl as his wife, Wexford would have taken her for no more than an adolescent. She had the smooth brow and bunchy cheeks of a child, the silken hair, the innocent eyes. She must have been married at sixteen, though she looked no more than that now.

Parker said with ferocious winks, "This gentleman's a doctor, come to tell us the poor lady's all right."

Nicky buried his face in his mother's shoulder.

"Quite all right," Wexford lied. "She'll be fine." They say the dead are well . . .

"You get along to Nanna's room then, Nicky, and she'll let you watch her T.V."

The tension lightened on his departure. "Thanks," said Parker. "I only hope it isn't going to have a bad effect on him, poor kid."

"Don't worry. He's too young to see newspapers, but you'll have to exercise a bit of censorship when it comes to the T.V. Now, Mr. Parker, I think you said Miss—er—Comfrey's father was in hospital. D'you know which hospital?"

"Stowerton. The infirmary. He had an accident last —when would it have been, Stell?"

"About May," said Stella Parker. "Miss Comfrey came down to see him, came in a taxi from the station, and when he saw her he rushed out of the house and fell over on the path and broke his hip. Just like that it happened. Her and the taximan, they took him to the hospital in the same taxi, and he's been there ever since. I never saw it. Mrs. Crown told me. Miss Comfrey'd been down once to see him since. She never did come much, did she, Brian?"

"Not more than once or twice a year," said Parker.

"I knew she was coming yesterday. Mrs. Crown told me. I saw her in the Post Office and she said Rhoda'd phoned to say she was coming on account of old Mr.

Comfrey'd had a stroke. But I never saw her, didn't really know her to speak to."

Burden said, "Who is Mrs. Crown?"

"Miss Comfrey's auntie. She lives in the next house to old Mr. Comfrey. She's the one you want to see."

"No doubt, but there's no one in."

"I tell you what," said Stella Parker who seemed to have twice her husband's grasp and intelligence, "I don't want to put myself forward, but I do read detective books, and if it's sort of background stuff you want, you couldn't do better than talk to Brian's gran. She's lived here all her life, she was born in one of those cottages."

"Your grandmother lives with you?"

"Helped us buy this place with her savings," said Parker, "and moved in with us. It works O.K., doesn't it, Stell? She's a wonder, my gran."

Wexford smiled and got up. "I may want to talk to her, but not tonight. You'll be notified about the inquest, Mr. Parker. It shouldn't be too much of an ordeal. Now, d'you know when Mrs. Crown will be home?"

"When the pubs turn out," said Parker.

"I think the infirmary next, Mike," said Wexford. "From the vague sort of time Crocker gave us, it's beginning to look to me as if Rhoda Comfrey was killed on her way back from visiting her father in hospital. She'd have used that footpath as a short cut from the bus stop."

"Visiting time at Stowerton's seven till eight in the evenings," said Burden. "We may be able to fix the time of death more accurately this way than by any post-mortem findings."

"The pub-oriented aunt should help us there. If this old boy's *compos mentis*, we'll get his daughter's London address from him."

"We'll also have to break the news," said Burden.

Departing visitors were queueing at the bus stop outside Stowerton Royal Infirmary. Had Rhoda Comfrey queued there on the previous night? It was ten past eight.

A man in the porter's lodge told them that James Albert Comfrey was a patient in Lytton Ward. They went along a corridor and up two flights of stairs. A pair of glass double doors, the entrance to Lytton Ward, were closed. As Wexford pushed them open, a young nurse of Malaysian or Thai origin popped up in their path and announced in a chirrup that they couldn't come in now.

"Police," said Burden. "We'd like to see the sister in charge."

"If you please, my dear," said Wexford, and the girl gave him a broad smile before hurrying off. "Do you have to be so bloody rude, Mike?"

She came back with Sister Lynch, a tall dark-haired Irishwoman in her late twenties.

"What can I do for you gentlemen?" She listened, clicked her tongue as Wexford gave her the bare details. "There's a terrible thing. A woman's not safe to walk abroad. And Miss Comfrey in here only last night to see her father."

"We'll have to see him, Sister."

"Not tonight you won't, Chief Inspector. I'm sure I'm sorry, but I couldn't allow it, not with the old gentlemen all settling down for the night. They'd none of them get a wink of sleep, and it's going off duty I am myself in ten minutes. I'll tell him myself tomorrow, though whether it'll sink in at all I doubt."

"He's senile?"

"There's a word, Chief Inspector, that I'm never knowing the meaning of. Eighty-five he is, and he's had a major stroke. Mostly he sleeps. If that's to be senile, senile he is. You'll be wasting your valuable time seeing him. I'll break it to him as best I can. Now would there be anything else?"

"Miss Comfrey's home address, please."

"Certainly." Sister Lynch beckoned to a dark-skinned girl who had appeared, pushing a trolley of drugs. "Would you get Miss Comfrey's home address from records, Nurse Mahmud?"

"Did you talk to Miss Comfrey last night, Sister?"

"No more than to say hallo and that the old gentleman was just the same. And I said good-bye to her too. She was talking to Mrs. Wells and they left together. Mrs. Wells's husband is in the next bed to Mr. Comfrey. Here's the address you were wanting. Thank you, nurse. Number one, Carlyle Villas, Forest Road, Kingsmarkham." Sister Lynch studied the card which had been handed to her. "No phone, I see."

"I'm afraid you've got Mr. Comfrey's address there," said Wexford. "It's his daughter's we want."

"But that is his daughter's, his and his daughter's."

Wexford shook his head. "No. She lived in London."

"It's the only one we have," said Sister Lynch, a slight edge to her voice. "As far as we know, Miss Comfrey lived in Kingsmarkham with her father."

"Then I'm afraid you were misled. Suppose you had had to get in touch with her—for instance, if her father had taken a turn for the worse—how would you have done so?"

"Notified her by letter. Or sent a messenger." Sister Lynch had begun to look huffy. He was questioning her efficiency. "That wouldn't have been necessary. Miss Comfrey phoned in almost every day. Last Thursday, now, she phoned on the very day her father had his stroke."

"And yet you say she hadn't a phone? Sister, I need that address. I shall have to see Mr. Comfrey."

Her eyes went to her watch and noted the time. She said very sharply, "Aren't I telling you, the poor old gentleman's no more than a vegetable at all? As for giving you an address, you'd as likely get an answer out of my little dog."

"Very well. In the absence of Miss Comfrey's address, I'll have Mrs. Wells's, please." This was provided, and Wexford said, "We'll come back tomorrow."

"You must suit yourselves. And now I'll take my leave of you."

Wexford murmured as they left, "There is nothing you could take from me that I would more willingly part withal," and then to Burden, who was smugly looking as if his early rudeness had been justified and he hoped his superior realised it, "We'll get it from the aunt. Odd, though, isn't it, her not giving her home address to the hospital?"

"Oh, I don't know. Underhand, but not odd. These old people can be a terrible drag. And it's always the women who are expected to look after them. I mean, old Comfrey'll be let out some time, and he won't be able to live on his own any more. A single woman and a daughter is a gift to all those busybody doctors and nurses and social workers. They'd seize on her. Wouldn't even consider expecting it of a son. If she gave them her real address, they'd pounce on that as a convalescent home for the old boy."

"You're the last person I thought I'd ever hear handing out Women's Lib propaganda," said Wexford. "Wonders will never cease. But doesn't it strike you that your theory only increases her chances of getting stuck with her father? They think she's on the spot, they think she lives with him already."

"There'll be an explanation. It isn't important, is it?"

"It's a departure from the norm, and that makes it important to me. I think Mrs. Wells next, Mike, and then back to Forest Road to wait for the aunt."

Mrs. Wells was seventy years old, slow of speech and rather confused. She had seen and spoken to Rhoda Comfrey twice before on her previous visits to the hospital, once in May and once in July. On the evening before they had got on the bus together outside the hospital at eight-fifteen. What had they talked about? Mrs. Wells thought it had mostly been about her husband's hip operation. Miss Comfrey hadn't said much, had seemed a bit nervous and uneasy. Worried about her father, Mrs. Wells thought. No, she didn't know her London address, believed in fact that she lived in Forest Road where she had said she was returning. Mrs. Wells had left the bus at the Kingsbrook Bridge, but her companion had remained on it, having a ticket to the next fare stage.

They returned to the police station. The weapon hadn't been found, and the house-to-house enquiry made by Loring, Marwood and Gates had produced negative results. No one in the cottages or the bungalows had heard or seen anything untoward on the previous evening. The inhabitants of the single detached house were away on holiday, and nobody had been working on the allotments. Rhoda Comfrey had been slightly known to everyone the three men had questioned, but only one had seen her on the previous day, and that had been when she left her father's house at about six-twenty to catch the bus for Stowerton. Her London address was unknown to any of the residents of Forest Road.

"I want you to get back there," Wexford said to Loring, "and wait for Mrs. Crown. I'm going home for an hour to get a bite to eat. When she comes in, call me on my home number."

3

Dora had been sewing, but the work had been laid aside, and he found her reading a novel. She got up immediately and brought him a bowl of soup, chicken salad, some fruit. He seldom talked about work at home, unless things got very tough. Home was a haven—Oh, what know they of harbours that sail not on the sea?—and he had fallen in love with and married the kind of woman who would give him one. But did she mind? Did she see herself as the one who waited and served while he lived? He had never thought much about it. Thinking of it now reawakened the anxiety that had lain dormant for the past three hours, pushed out of mind by greater urgencies.

"Hear any more from Sylvia?" he said.

"Neil came round for the Teddy bear. Ben wouldn't go to sleep without it." She touched his arm, then rested her hand on his wrist. "You mustn't worry about her. She's grown-up. She has to cope with her own problems."

"Your son's your son," said her husband, "till he gets him a wife, but your daughter's your daughter the whole of your life."

"There goes the phone." She sighed, but not rebelliously. "I have measured out my life in telephone bells."

"Don't wait up for me," said Wexford.

It was dark now, ten minutes to eleven, the wide sky covered all over with stars. And the moonlight was strong enough to cast bold shadows of tree and gate and pillar box along the length of Forest Road. A single street lamp shone up by the stone wall, and lights were on all over 2, Carlyle Villas, though the other houses were in darkness. He rang the bell on the reeded glass and wrought-iron front door.

"Mrs. Crown?"

He had expected a negative answer because this woman was much younger than he had thought she would be. Only a few years older than he. But she said yes, she was, and asked him what he wanted. She smelt of gin and had about her the reckless air—no apparent fear of him or cautiousness or suspicion—that drink brings, though this might have been habitual with her. He told her who he was, and she let him in. There, in a cluttered bizarre living room, he broke the news to her, speaking gently and considerately but all the time sensing that gentleness and consideration weren't needed here.

"Well, fancy," she said. "What a thing to happen! Rhoda, of all people. That's given me a bit of a shock, that has. A drink is called for. Want one?" Wexford shook his head. She helped herself from a gin bottle that stood on a limed oak sideboard whose surface was covered with drips and smears and ring marks. "I won't make a show of grief. We weren't close. Where did you say it happened? Down the footpath? You won't see me down there in a hurry, I can tell you."

She was like the room they were in, small and overdressed in bright colours and none too clean. The stretch nylon covers on her chairs were of a slightly duller yellow than the tight dress she wore, and unlike it, they were badly marked with cigarette burns. But all were disfigured with the same sort of liquor splashes and food stains. Mrs. Crown's hair was of the same colour and texture as the dried grasses that stood everywhere in green and yellow vases, pale and thin and brittle but defiantly gold. She lit a cigarette and left it hanging in her mouth which was painted, as her niece's had been, to match her fingernails.

"I haven't yet been able to inform your brother," Wexford said. "It would appear he's not up to it."

"Brother-in-*law*, if you don't mind," said Mrs. Crown. "He's not my brother, the old devil."

"Ah, yes," said Wexford. "Now, Mrs. Crown, it's getting late and I don't want to keep you up, but I'd like to know what you can tell me of Miss Comfrey's movements yesterday."

She stared at him, blowing smoke through her sharp nose. "What's that got to do with some maniac stabbing her? Killed her for her money, didn't he? She was always loaded, was Rhoda." Horrifyingly, she added, with a Wife of Bath look, remembering the old dance, "Wouldn't be for sex, not so likely."

Wexford didn't take her up on that one. He said repressively, "You saw her yesterday?"

"She phoned me Friday to say she'd be coming. Thought I might get bothered if I saw lights on next door, not expecting anyone to be there, if you see what I mean. God knows why she put herself out. I was amazed. Picked up the phone and she says, 'Hallo, Lilian. I wonder if you know who this is?' Of course I knew. I'd know that deep voice of hers anywhere and that put-on accent. She never got that from her mum and dad. But you don't want to know all that. She came in a taxi yesterday about one. All dressed-up she was, but miserable as sin. She was always down in the mouth when she came here, made no secret she hated the place, far cry from the way she sounded on the phone, all cocky, if you know what I mean. Sure you won't have a drink? I think I'll have a drop more."

A good deal more than a drop of neat gin in her glass, Lilian Crown perched on the sofa arm and swung her legs. The calves were shapeless with varicose veins, but she still kept the high instep, the dancing foot, of one who has led a riotous youth. "She never came in here till a quarter past six. 'Feel like coming with me, Lilian?' she said, knowing damn well I wouldn't. I told her I'd got a date with my gentleman friend, which was the honest truth, but I could tell she didn't like it, always was jealous. 'When'll you be back?' she said. 'I'll come in and tell you how he is.' 'All right,' I said, doing my best to be pleasant, though I never had any time for him or her after my poor sister went. 'I'll be in by ten,' I said, but she never came and no lights came on. Gone straight back to London, I thought, knowing her, never dreaming a thing like that had happened."

Wexford nodded. "I'll very likely want to see you again, Mrs. Crown. In the meantime, would you give me Miss Comfrey's London address?"

"I haven't got it."

"You mean you don't *know* it?"

"That's what I mean. Look, I live next door to the old devil, sure I do, but that's convenience, that is. I came here for my sister's sake, and after she went I just stopped on. But that doesn't mean we were close. As a matter of fact, him and me, we weren't on speaking terms. As for Rhoda—well, I won't speak ill of the dead. She was my sister's girl, when all's said and done, but we never did get on. She left home must be twenty years ago, and if I've set eyes on her a dozen times since, that's it. She'd no call to give me her address or her phone number, and I'm sure I wouldn't have asked for it. Look, if I'd got it I'd give it to you, wouldn't I? I'd have no call not to."

"At least, I suppose you know what she did for a living?"

"In business, she was," said Lilian Crown. "Got her own business." Bitterness pinched her face. "Money stuck to Rhoda, always did. And she hung on to it. None of it came my way or *his*. He's a proper old devil, but he's her dad, isn't he?"

A woman who had said she wouldn't speak ill of the dead . . . Wexford went home, building up in his mind a picture of what Rhoda Comfrey had been. A middle-aged, well-off, successful woman, probably self-employed; a woman who had disliked the town of her origins because it held for her painful associations; who liked her privacy and had kept, insofar as she could, her address to herself; a clever, cynical, hard-bitten woman, indifferent to this country world's opinion, and owing to her unpleasant old father no more than a bare duty. Still, it was too early for this sort of speculation. In the morning they would have a warrant to search Mr. Comfrey's house. The address, the nature of her business, would be discovered, and Rhoda Comfrey's life unfolded. Already Wexford had a feeling—one of those illogical intuitive feelings the Chief Constable so much disliked—that the motive for her murder lay in that London life.

Kingsmarkham Police Station had been built about fifteen years before, and the conservative townsfolk had been shocked by the appearance of this stark white box with its flat roof and wide picture windows. But a decade and a half had tripled the size of the saplings around it so that now its severity was half-screened by birches and laburnums. Wexford had his office on the second floor: buttercup-yellow walls with maps on them and a decorous calendar of Sussex views, a new blue carpet, his own desk of dark red rosewood that belonged to him personally and not to the Mid-Sussex Constabulary. The big window afforded him a fine view of the High Street, of higgledy-piggledy roof tops, of green meadows beyond. This morning, Wednesday, 10 August, it was wide open and the air-conditioning switched off. Another lovely day, exactly what the clear sky and stars and bright moon of the previous night had promised.

Since he had looked in first thing in the morning and left again for Stowerton Royal Infirmary, the clothes Rhoda Comfrey had been wearing had been sent up and left on the desk. Wexford threw down beside them the early editions of the evening papers he had just picked up. Middle-aged spinsters, even when stabbed to death, were apparently not news, and neither paper had allotted to this murder more than a couple of paragraphs on an inside page. He sat down by the window to cool down, for the front aspect of the police station was still in shade.

James Albert Comfrey. They had drawn cretonne curtains printed with flowers round the old man's bed. His hands moved like crabs, gnarled and crooked, across the sheet. Sometimes they plucked at a tuft of wool on the red blanket, then they parted and crawled back, only to begin again on their journey. His mouth was open, he breathed stertorously. In the strong tough yet enfeebled face, Wexford had seen the lineaments of the daughter—the big nose, long upper lip and cliff-like chin.

"Like I said," said Sister Lynch, "it never meant a thing to him when I passed on the news. There's little that registers at all."

"Mr. Comfrey," said Wexford, approaching the bed.

"Sure, and you may as well save your breath."

"I'd like to have a look in that locker."

"I can't have that," said Sister Lynch.

"I have a warrant to search his house." Wexford was beginning to lose his patience. "D'you think I couldn't get one to search a cupboard?"

"What's my position going to be if there's a come-back?"

"You mean *he's* going to complain to the hospital board?" Without wasting any more time, Wexford had opened the lower part of the locker. It contained nothing but a pair of slippers and a rolled-up dressing gown. Irish ire making itself apparent behind him in little sharp exhalations, he shook out the dressing gown and felt in its pockets. Nothing. He rolled it up again. An infringement of privacy? he thought. The gown was made of red towelling with 'Stowerton Infirmary' worked in white cotton on its hem. Perhaps James Comfrey no longer possessed anything of his own.

He did. In the drawer above the cupboard was a set of dentures in a plastic box and a pair of glasses. Impossible to imagine this man owning an address book. There was nothing of that sort in the drawer, nothing else at all but a scrap of folded tissue.

So he had come away, baulked and wondering. But the house itself would yield that address, and if it didn't those newspaper accounts, meagre as they were, would rouse the London friends and acquaintances, employers or employees, who must by now have missed her.

He turned his attention to the clothes. It was going to be a day of groping through other people's possessions —such closets to search, such alcoves to importune! Rhoda Comfrey's dress and jacket, shoes and underwear, were unremarkable, the medium-priced garments of a woman who had retained a taste for bright colours and fussy trimmings into middle age. The shoes were a little distorted by feet that had spread. No perfume clung to the fabric of dress and slip. He was examining labels which told him only that the shoes came from one of a chain of shops whose name had been a household word for a quarter of a century, that the clothes might have been bought in any Oxford Street or Knightsbridge emporium, when there came a knock at the door.

The head of Dr. Crocker appeared. "What seems to be the trouble?" said the doctor very breezily.

They were lifelong friends, having known each other since their school days when Leonard Crocker had been in the first form and Reginald Wexford in the sixth. And it had sometimes been Wexford's job— how he had loathed it!—to shepherd home to the street next his own in Pomfret, the mischievous recalcitrant infant. Now they were both getting on in years, but the mischievousness remained. Wexford was in no mood for it this morning.

"What d'you think?" he growled. "Guess."

Crocker walked over to the desk and picked up one of the shoes. "The old man's my patient, you know."

"No, I don't know. And I hope to God you haven't come here just to be mysterious about it. I've had some of that nonsense from you before. 'The secrets of the confessional' and 'a doctor's like a priest' and all that rubbish."

Crocker ignored this. "Old Comfrey used to come to my surgery regularly every Tuesday night. Nothing

wrong with him bar old age till he broke his hip.
These old people, they like to come in for a chat. I just
thought you might be interested."

"I am, of course, if it's interesting."

"Well, it's the daughter that's dead and he was always on about his daughter. How she'd left him all on
his own since her mother died and neglected him and
didn't come to see him from one year's end to the
next. He was really quite articulate about it. Now, how
did he describe her?"

"A thwart disnatured torment?"

The doctor raised his eyebrows. "That's good, but it
doesn't sound old Comfrey's style. I've heard it somewhere before."

"Mm," said Wexford. "No doubt you have. But
let's not go into the comminations of Lear on his
thankless child. You will, of course, know the thankless
child's address."

"London."

"Oh, really! If anyone else says that to me I'll put
them on a charge for obstruction. You mean even *you*
don't know where in London? For God's sake, Len,
this old boy's eighty-five. Suppose you'd been called
out to him and found him at death's door? How would
you have got in touch with his next of kin?"

"He wasn't at death's door. People don't have death-
beds like that any more, Reg. They get ill, they linger,
they go into hospital. The majority of people die in
hospital these days. During the whole long painful
process we'd have got her address."

"Well, you didn't," Wexford snapped. "The hospital
hasn't got it now. How about that? I have to have that
address."

"It'll be at old Comfrey's place," said Crocker easily.

"I just hope so. I'm going over there now to find it if
it's findable."

The doctor jumped down from his perch on the edge
of the desk. With one of those flashbacks to his youth,

to his school days, he said on an eager note, "Can I come too?"

"I suppose so. But I don't want you cavorting about and getting in everyone's way."

"Thanks very much," said Crocker in mock dudgeon. "Who do you think the popularity polls show to be the most respected members of the community? General practitioners."

"I knew it wasn't cops," said Wexford.

4

The house smelt as he had thought it would, of the old person's animal-vegetable-mineral smell, sweat, cabbage and camphor.

"What did moths live on before man wore woollen clothes?"

"Sheep, I suppose," said the doctor.

"But do sheep have moths?"

"God knows. This place is a real tip, isn't it?"

They were turning out drawers in the two downstairs rooms. Broken pens and pencils, dried-out ink bottles, sticking plaster, little glass jars full of pins, dead matches, nails, nuts and bolts, screws of thread; an assortment of keys, a pair of dirty socks full of holes, pennies and threepenny bits from the old currency, pieces of string, a broken watch, some marbles and some dried peas; a five-amp electric plug, milk bottle tops, the lid of a paint tin encrusted with blue from the front door, cigarette cards, picture hangers and an ancient shaving brush.

"Nice little breeding ground for anthrax," said Crocker, and he pocketed a dozen or so boxes and bottles of pills that were ranged on top of the chest. "I may as well dispose of this lot while I'm here. They won't chuck them out, no matter how often you tell them. Though why they should be so saving when they get them for free in the first place, I never will know."

The footfalls of Burden, Loring and Gates could be heard overhead. Wexford knelt down, opened the bottle drawer. Underneath a lot of scattered mothballs, more socks redolent of cheesy mustiness, and a half-empty packet of bird seed, he found an oval picture frame lying face-downwards. He turned it over and looked at a photograph of a young woman with short dark hair, strong jaw, long upper lip, biggish nose.

"I suppose that's her," he said to the doctor.

"Wouldn't know. I never saw her till she was dead and she didn't look much like that then. It's the spitting image of the old man, though, isn't it? It's her all right."

Wexford said thoughtfully and a little sadly, remembering the overly made-up, raddled face, "It does look like her. It's just that it was taken a long time ago." And yet she hadn't looked sad. The dead face, if it were possible to say such a thing, had looked almost pleased with itself. "We'll try upstairs," he said.

There was no bathroom in the house, and the only lavatory was outside in the garden. The stairs were not carpeted but covered with linoleum. Burden came out of the front bedroom which was James Comfrey's.

"Proper old glory hole in there. D'you know, there's not a book in the house, and not a letter or a postcard either."

"The spare room," said Crocker.

It was a bleak little place, the walls papered in a print of faded pink and mauve sweet peas, the bare floorboards stained dark brown, the thin curtains whitish now but showing faintly the remains of a pink pattern. On the white cotton counterpane that covered the single bed lay a freshly pressed skirt in a navy-checked synthetic material, a blue nylon blouse and a pair of tights still in their plastic wrapping. Apart from a wall cupboard and a very small chest of drawers, there was no other furniture. On the chest was a small suitcase. Wexford looked inside it and found a pair of cream silk pyjamas of better quality than any of Rhoda Comfrey's daytime wear, sandals of the kind that consist only of a rubber sole and rubber thong, and a sponge bag. That was all. The cupboard was empty as were the drawers of the chest.

The closets had been searched and the alcoves importuned in vain.

Wexford said hotly to Crocker and Burden, "This is unbelievable. She doesn't give her address to her aunt or the hospital where her father is or to her father's doctor or his neighbours. It's not written down anywhere in his house, he hasn't got it with him in the hospital. No doubt, it was in his head where it's now either locked in or knocked out. What the hell was she playing at?"

"Possum," said the doctor.

Wexford gave a snort. "I'm going across the road," he said. "Mind you leave the place as you found it. That means untidying anything you've tidied up." He grinned snidely at Crocker. It made a change for him to order the doctor about, for the boot was usually on the other foot. "And get Mrs. Crown formally to identify the body, will you, Mike? I wish you joy of her."

Nicky Parker opened the door of Bella Vista, his mother close behind him in the hall. Again the reassuring game was played for the child's benefit and Wexford passed off as a doctor. Well, why not? Weren't doctors the most respected members of the community? A baby was crying somewhere, and Stella Parker looked harassed.

"Would it be convenient," he said politely, "for me to have a chat with your—er, grandmother-in-law?"

She said she was sure it would, and Wexford was led through to a room at the back of the house. Sitting in an armchair, on her lap a colander containing peas

that she was shelling, sat one of the oldest people he
had ever seen in his life.

"Nanna, this is the police inspector."

"How do you do, Mrs.—?"

"Nanna's called Parker too, the same as us."

She was surrounded by preparations for the family's
lunch. On the floor, on one side of her chair, stood a
saucepanful of potatoes in water, the bowl of peelings in
water beside it. Four cooking apples awaited her attention. Pastry was made, kneaded, and set on a plate.
This, apparently, was one of the ways in which she, at
her extreme age, contributed to the household manage-
ment. Wexford remembered how Parker had called his
grandmother a wonder, and he began to see why.

For a moment she took no notice of him, exercising
perhaps the privilege of matriarchal eld. Stella Parker
left them and shut the door. The old woman split open
the last of her pods, an enormous one, and said as if
they were old acquaintances:

"When I was a girl they used to say, if you find nine
peas in a pod put it over your door and the next man to
come in will be your own true love." She scattered the
nine peas into the full colander, wiped her greened fingers on her apron.

"Did you ever do it?" said Wexford.

"What d'you say? Speak up."

"Did you ever do it?"

"Not me. Didn't need to. I'd been engaged to Mr.
Parker since we was both fifteen. Sit down, young man.
You're too tall to be up on your legs."

Wexford was amused and absurdly flattered. "Mrs.
Parker . . ." he began on a bellow, but she interrupted
him with what was very likely a favourite question.

"How old d'you think I am?"

There are only two periods in a woman's life when
she hopes to be taken for older than she is, under sixteen and over ninety. In each case the error praises a
certain achievement. But still he was wary.

She didn't wait for an answer. "Ninety-two," she said, "and I still do the veg and make my own bed and do my room. And I looked after Brian and Nicky when Stell was in the hospital having Katrina. I was only eighty-nine then, though. Eleven children I've had and reared them all. Six of them gone now." She levelled at him a girl's blue eyes in nests of wrinkles. "It's not good to see your children go before you do, young man." Her face was white bone in a sheath of crumpled parchment. "Brian's dad was my youngest, and he's been gone two years come November. Only fifty, he was. Still, Brian and Stell have been wonderful to me. They're a wonder, they are, the pair of them." Her mind, drifting through the past, the ramifications of her family, returned to him, this stranger who must have come for something. "What were you wanting? Police, Stell said." She sat back, put the colander on the floor, and folded her hands. "Rhoda Comfrey, is it?"

"Your grandson told you?"

"Course he did. Before he ever told you." She was proud that she enjoyed the confidence of the young, and she smiled. But the smile was brief. Archaically, she said, "She was wickedly murdered."

"Yes, Mrs. Parker. I believe you knew her well?"

"As well as my own children. She used to come and see me every time she come down here. Rather see me than her dad, she would."

At last, he thought. "Then you'll be able to tell me her address?"

"Speak up, will you?"

"Her address in London?"

"Don't know it. What'd I want to know that for? I've not written a letter in ten years and I've only been to London twice in my life."

He had wasted his time coming here, and he couldn't afford to waste time.

"I can tell you all about her, though," said Mrs.

Parker. "Everything you'll want to know. And about the family. Nobody can tell you like I can. You've come to the right place for that."

"Mrs. Parker, I don't think . . ." That I care? That it matters? What he wanted at this stage was an address, not a biography, especially not one told with meanderings and digressions. But how to cut short without offence a woman of ninety-two whose deafness made interruption virtually impossible? He would have to listen and hope it wouldn't go on too long. Besides, she had already begun . . .

"They come here when Rhoda was a little mite. An only child she was, and used to play with my two youngest. A poor feeble thing was Agnes Comfrey, didn't know how to stand up for herself, and Mr. Comfrey was a real terror. I don't say he hit her or Rhoda, but he ruled them with a rod of iron just the same." She rapped out sharply, "You come across that Mrs. Crown yet?"

"Yes," said Wexford, "but . . ." Oh, not the aunt, he thought, not that bypath. She hadn't heard him.

"You will. A crying scandal to the whole neighbourhood, she is. Used to come here visiting her sister when her first husband was alive. Before the war, that was, and she was a real fly-by-night even then, though she never took to drink till he was killed at Dunkirk. She had this baby about three months after—I dare say it was his all right, give her the benefit of the doubt—but it was one of them mongols, poor little love. John, they called him. Her and him come to live here with the Comfreys. Aggie used to come over to me in a terrible state of worry about what Lilian got up to and tried to keep dark, and Jim Comfrey threatening to throw her out.

"Well, the upshot of it was she met this Crown in the nick of time and they took the house next door when they was married on account of it had been empty all through the war. And d'you know what she done then?"

Wexford shook his head and stared at the pyramid of peas which were having a mesmeric effect on him.

"I'll tell you. She had little John put in a home. Have you ever heard the like, for a mother to do a thing like that? Sweet affectionate little love he was too, the way them mongols are, and loved Rhoda, and she taking him out with her, not a bit ashamed."

"She'd have been how old then, Mrs. Parker?" Wexford said for something to say. It was a mistake because he didn't really care, and he had to bawl it twice more before she heard.

"Twelve, she was, when he was born, and sixteen when Lilian had him put away. She was at the County High School, and Mr. Comfrey wanted to take her away when she was fourteen like you could in them days. The headmistress herself, Miss Fowler that was, come to the house personally herself to beg him let Rhoda stay on, her being so bright. Well, he gave way for a bit, but he wasn't having her go on to no college, made her leave at sixteen, wanted her money, he said, the old skinflint."

It was very hot, and the words began to roll over Wexford, only half-heard. Just the very usual unhappy tale of the mean-spirited working-class parent who values cash in hand more than the career in the future. "Got shop work—wanted to better herself, did Rhoda —always shut up in that back bedroom reading— taught herself French—went to typing classes—" How the hell was he going to get that address? Trace her through those clothes, those antique shoes? Not a hope. The sharp old voice cackled on. "Nothing to look at— never had a boy—that Lilian always at her—'When you going to get yourself a boy friend, Rhoda?'—got to be a secretary—poor thing, she used to get herself up like Lilian, flashy clothes and high heels and paint all over her face." He'd have to get help from the Press: *Do You Know This Woman?* On the strength of that photograph? "Aggie got cancer—never went to the doctor till it was too late—had an operation, but it wasn't no use—she passed on and poor Rhoda was left with the old man—"

Well, he wasn't going to allow publication of photos of her dead face, never had done that and never would. If only Mrs. Parker would come to an end, if only she hadn't about twenty years still to go! "And would have stayed, I dare say—been a slave to him—stayed forever but for getting all that money—tied to him hand and foot—"

"What did you say?"

"I'm the one that's deaf, young man," said Mrs. Parker.

"I know, I'm sorry. But what was that about coming into money?"

"You want to listen when you're spoke to, not go off in daydreams. She didn't come into money, she won it. On the pools, it was one of the office what-d'you-call-its."

"Syndicates?"

"I dare say. Old Jim Comfrey, he thought he was in clover. 'My ship's come in,' he says to my eldest son. But he was wrong there. Rhoda upped and walked out on him, and so much for the house he was going to have and the car and all."

"How much was it?"

"How much was what? What she won? Thousands and thousands. She never said and I wouldn't ask. She come round to my place one afternoon—I was living up the road then—and she'd got a big case all packed. Just thirty, she was, and twenty years ago nearly to the day. She had the same birthday as me, you see, August the fifth, and forty-two years between us. 'I'm leaving, Auntie Vi,' she says, 'going to London to seek my fortune,' and she gives me the address of some hotel and says would I have all her books packed up and sent on to her? Fat chance of that. Jim Comfrey burned the lot of them down in the garden. I can see her now like it was yesterday, in them high heels she couldn't walk in properly and a dress all frills, and beads all over her and fingernails like she'd dipped them in red paint and . . ."

"You didn't see her yesterday, did you?" Wexford yelled rapidly. "I mean, the day before yesterday?"

"No. Didn't know she was here. She'd have come, though, if it wasn't for some wicked . . ."

"What was she going to do in London, Mrs. Parker?"

"Be a reporter on a paper. That's what she wanted. She was secretary to the editor of the *Gazette* and she used to write bits for them too. I told you all that only you wasn't listening."

Puzzled, he said, "But Mrs. Crown said she was in business."

"All I can say is, if you believe her, you'll believe anything. Rhoda got to be a reporter and did well for herself, had a nice home, she used to tell me, and what with the money she'd won and her wages . . ."

He bellowed, "What newspaper, d'you know? Whereabouts was this home of hers?"

Mrs. Parker drew herself up, assuming a duchessy dignity. She said rather frigidly, "Lord knows, I hope you'll never get to be deaf, young man. But maybe you'll never understand unless you do. Half the things folks say to you go over your head, and you can't keep stopping them to ask them what? Can you? They think you're going mental. Rhoda used to say she'd written a bit here and a bit there, and gone to this place or that, and bought things for her home and whatnot, and how nice it was and what nice friends she'd got. I liked to hear her talk, I liked her being friendly with an old woman, but I know better than to think I'm like to follow half the things she *said*."

Defeated, flattened, bludgeoned and nearly stunned, Wexford got up. "I must go, Mrs. Parker."

"I won't quarrel with that," she said tartly, and showing no sign of fatigue. "You've fair worn me out, roaring at me like a blooming bull." She handed him the colander and the potatoes. "You can make yourself useful and give these to Stell. And tell her to bring me in a pie dish."

5

Had she perhaps been a free-lance journalist?

At the press conference Wexford gave that afternoon, he asked this question of Harry Wild, of the *Kingsmarkham Courier,* and of the only reporter any national newspaper had bothered to send. Neither of them had heard of her in this connection, though Harry vaguely remembered a plain-featured dark girl called Comfrey who, twenty years before, had been secretary to the editor of the now defunct *Gazette.*

"And now," Wexford said to Burden, "we'll adjourn to the Olive for a well-earned drink. See if you can find Crocker. He's about somewhere, dying to get the low-down on the medical report."

The doctor was found, and they made their way to the Olive and Dove where they sat outside at a table in the little garden. It had been the sort of summer that seldom occurs in England, the sort foreigners believe never occurs, though the Englishman of middle age can look back and truthfully assert there have been three or four such in his lifetime. Weeks, months, of undimmed sunshine had pushed geraniums up to five feet and produced fuchsias of a size and profusion only generally seen inside a heated greenhouse. None of the three men wore a jacket, but the doctor alone sported a T-shirt, a short-sleeved adolescent garment in which he made his rounds and entranced his female patients.

Wexford drank white wine, very dry and as cold as

the Olive was able to produce it which, tonight, was
around blood heat. The occasional beer was for when
Crocker, a stern medical mentor, wasn't around. It was
a while now since the chief inspector had suffered a
mild thrombosis, but any excesses, as the doctor never
tired of telling him, could easily lead to another.

He began by congratulating his friend on the accuracy of his on-the-spot estimate of the time of death.
The eminent pathologist who had conducted the
post-mortem had put it at between seven and nine-
thirty.

"Eight-thirty's the most probable," he said, "on her
way home from the bus stop." He sipped his warm
wine. "She was a strong healthy woman—until someone put a knife in her. One stab wound pierced a lung
and the other the left ventricle. No signs of disease, no
abnormalities. Except one. I think in these days you
could call it an abnormality."

"What d'you mean?" said Crocker.

"She was a virgin."

Burden, that strait-laced puritan, jerked up his head.
"Good heavens, she was an unmarried woman, wasn't
she? Things have come to a pretty pass, I must say, if
a perfectly proper condition for a single woman is
called abnormal."

"I suppose you must say it, Mike," said Wexford
with a sigh, "but I wish you wouldn't. I agree that a
hundred years ago, fifty years ago, even twenty, such a
thing wouldn't be unusual in a woman of fifty, but it is
now."

"Unusual in a woman of fif*teen*, if you ask me,"
said the doctor.

"Look at it this way. She was only thirty when she
left home, and that was just at the beginning of the
stirrings of the permissive society. She had some money. Presumably, she lived alone without any kind of
chaperonage. All right, she was never very attractive or
charming, but she wasn't repulsive, she wasn't de-

formed. Isn't it very strange indeed that in those first
ten years at least she never had one love affair, not even
one adventure for the sake of the experience?"

"Frigid," said Crocker. "Everyone's supposed to be
rolling about from bed to bed these days, but you'd
be surprised how many people just aren't interested in
sex. Women especially. Some of them put up a good
showing, they really try, but they'd much rather be
watching the T.V."

"So old Acton was right, was he? 'A modest woman'," Wexford quoted, " 'seldom desires any sexual
gratification for herself. She submits to her husband
but only to please him and, but for the desire for ma-
ternity, would far rather be relieved from his atten-
tions.' "

Burden drained his glass and made a face like someone who has taken unpalatable medicine. He had been
a policeman for longer than Rhoda Comfrey had been
free of parental ties, had seen human nature in every
possible seamy or sordid aspect, yet his experience had
scarcely at all altered his attitude towards sexual matters. He was still one of those people whose feelings
about sex are grossly ambivalent. For him it was both
dirty and holy. He had never read that quaint Victo-
rian manual, Dr. Acton's *Functions and Disorders of
the Reproductive Organs,* male-oriented, prudish, repressive and biologically very wide of the mark, but
it was for such as he that it had been written. Now,
while Wexford and the doctor—who for some reason
beyond his comprehension seemed to know the work
well—were quoting from it with scathing laughter and
casting up of eyes, he said brusquely, interrupting them,

"In my opinion, this has absolutely nothing to do
with Rhoda Comfrey's murder."

"Very likely not, Mike. It seems a small point when
we don't even know where she lived or how she lived
or who her friends were. But I hope all that will be
solved tomorrow."

"What's so special about tomorrow?"

"I think we shall see that this rather dull little back-woods killing will have moved from the inside pages to be front-page news. I've been very frank with the news-papers—mostly via Harry Wild who'll scoop a packet in linage—and I think I've given them the sort of thing they like. I've also given them that photograph, for what it's worth. I'll be very much surprised if tomorrow morning we don't see headlines such as *Murdered Woman Led Double Life* and *What Was Stabbed Woman's Secret?*"

"You mean," said Burden, "that some neighbour of hers or employer or the man who delivers her milk will see it and let us know?"

Wexford nodded. "Something like that. I've given the Press a number for anyone with information to ring. You see, that neighbour or employer may have read about her death today without its occurring to them that we're still in ignorance of her address."

The doctor went off to get fresh drinks. "All the nuts will be on the blower," said Burden. "All the men whose wives ran away in 1956; all the paranoiacs and sensation-mongers."

"That can't be helped. We have to sort out the sheep from the goats. God knows, we've done it before often enough."

The newspapers, as he put it, did him proud. They went, as always, too far with headlines more bizarre than those he had predicted. If the photograph, touched up out of recognition, struck no chords, he was sure the text must. Rhoda Comfrey's past was there, the circum-stances of her Kingsmarkham life, the history of her association with the old *Gazette*, the details of her fath-er's illness. Mrs. Parker and Mrs. Crown had apparent-ly not been so useless after all.

By nine the phone began to ring.

For Wexford, his personal phone had been ringing throughout the night, but those calls had been from newspapermen wanting more details and all ready to assure him that Rhoda Comfrey hadn't worked for *them*. In Fleet Street she was unknown. Reaching the station early, he set Loring to trying all the London local papers, while he himself waited for something to come from the special line. Every call that had the slightest hint of genuineness about it was to be relayed to him.

Burden, of course, had been right. All the nuts were on the blower. There was the spiritualist whose sister had died fifteen years before and who was certain Rhoda Comfrey must have been that sister reincarnated; the son whose mother had abandoned him when he was twelve; the husband, newly released from a mental hospital, whose wife that he declared missing came and took the receiver from him with embarrassed apologies; the seer who offered to divine the dead woman's address from the aura of her clothes. None of these calls even reached Wexford's sanctum, though he was told of them. Personally he took the call from George Rowlands, former editor of the *Gazette,* who had nothing to tell him but that Rhoda had been a good secretary with the makings of a feature-writer. Every well-meant and apparently sane call he took, but the day passed without anything to justify his optimism. Friday came, and with it the inquest.

It was quickly adjourned, and nothing much came out of it but a reproof for Brian Parker from an unsympathetic coroner. This was a court, not a child-guidance clinic, said the coroner, managing also to imply that the paucity of evidence was somehow due to Parker's having rearranged Rhoda Comfrey's clothes.

The phone calls still came sporadically in on the Saturday, but not one caller claimed to know Rhoda Comfrey by name or said he or she had lived next door to her or worked with her. No bank manager phoned to say she had an account at his bank, no landlord to say that she paid him rent.

"This," said Wexford, "is ridiculous. Am I supposed to believe she lived in a tent in Hyde Park?"

"Of course it has to be that she was living under an assumed name." Burden stood at the window and watched the bus from Stowerton pause at the stop, let off a woman passenger not unlike Rhoda Comfrey, then move off towards Forest Road. "I thought the papers were doing their usual hysterical stuff when they printed all that about her secret life." He looked at Wexford, raising his eyebrows. "I thought you were too."

"My usual hysterical stuff. Thanks very much."

"I meant melodramatic," said Burden, as if that mitigated the censure. "But they weren't. You weren't. Why would she behave like that?"

"For the usual melodramatic reason. Because she didn't want the people who knew Rhoda Comfrey to know what Rhoda Comfrey was up to. Espionage, drug-running, protection rackets, a call-girl ring. It's bound to be something like that."

"Look, I didn't mean you always exaggerate. I've said I was wrong, haven't I? As a matter of fact, the call-girl idea did come into my mind. Only she was a bit old for that and nothing much to look at and—well . . ."

"Well, what? She was the only virgin prostitute in London, was she? It's a new line, Mike, it's an idea. It's a refreshing change in these dissolute times. I can think of all sorts of fascinating possibilities in that one, only I wouldn't like to burn your chaste ears. Shall we try to be realistic?"

"I always do," said Burden gloomily. He sat down and rested his elbows on Wexford's desk. "She's been dead since Monday night, and it's Sunday now, and we don't even know where she lived. It seems hopeless."

"That's not being realistic, that's defeatist. She can't be traced through her name or her description, therefore she must be traced by other means. In a negative sort of way, all this has shown us something. It's shown us that her murder is connected with that other life of hers. A secret life is almost always a life founded on something illicit or illegal. In the course of it she did something which gave someone a reason to kill her."

"You mean we can't dismiss the secret life and concentrate on the circumstantial and concrete evidence we have?"

"Like what? No weapon, no witnesses, no smell of a motive?" Wexford hesitated and said more slowly, "She seldom came back here, but she had been coming once or twice a year. The local people knew her by sight, knew who she was. Therefore, I don't think this is a case of someone returning home after a long absence and being recognised—to put it melodramatically, Mike—by an old enemy. Nor was her real life here or her work or her interests or her involvements. Those, whatever they were, she left behind in London."

"You don't think the circumstances point to local knowledge?"

"I don't. I say her killer knew she was coming here and followed her, though not, possibly, with premeditation to kill. He or she came from London, having known her in that other life of hers. So never mind the locals. We have to come to grips with the London life, and I've got an idea how to do it. Through that wallet she had in her handbag."

"I'm listening," said Burden with a sigh.

"I've got it here." Wexford produced the wallet from a drawer in his desk. "See the name printed in gold on the inside? Silk and Whitebeam."

"Sorry, it doesn't mean a thing to me."

"They're a very exclusive leather shop in Jermyn Street. That wallet's new. I think there's a chance they might remember who they sold it to, and I'm sending Loring up first thing in the morning to ask them. Rhoda Comfrey had a birthday last week. If she didn't buy it herself, I'm wondering what are the chances of someone else having bought it for her as a gift."

"For a *woman?*"

"Why not? If she was in need of a wallet. Women

carry banknotes as much as we do. The days of giving women a bottle of perfume or a brooch are passing, Mike. They are very nearly the people now. *Sic transit gloria mundi*."

"*Sic transit gloria* Sunday, if you ask me," said Burden.

Wexford laughed. His subordinate and friend could still surprise him.

6

As soon as he had let himself into his house, Dora came out from the kitchen, beckoned him into it and shut the door.

"Sylvia's here."

There is nothing particularly odd or unusual about a married daughter visiting her mother on a Sunday afternoon, and Wexford said, "Why shouldn't she be? What d'you mean?"

"She's left Neil. She just walked out after lunch and came here."

"Are you saying she's seriously *left Neil?* Just like that? She's walked out on her husband and come home to mother? I can't believe it."

"Darling, it's true. Apparently they've been having a continuous quarrel ever since Wednesday night. He promised to take her to Paris for a week in September —his sister was going to have the children—and now he says he can't go, he's got to go to Sweden on business. Well, in the resulting row Sylvia said she couldn't stand it any longer, being at home all day with the children and never having a break, and he'd have to get an *au pair* so that she could go out and train for something. So he said—though I think she's exaggerating there—that he wasn't going to pay a girl wages to do what it was his wife's job to do. She'd only train for something and then not be able to get a job because of the unemployment. Anyway, all this developed into a great analysis of their marriage and the role men have made women play and how she was sacrificing her whole life. You can imagine. So this morning she told him that if she was only a nurse and a housekeeper, she'd go and be a nurse and housekeeper with her parents—and here she is."

"Where is she now?"

"In the living room, and Robin and Ben are in the garden. I don't know how much they realise. Darling, don't be harsh with her."

"When have I ever been harsh with my children? I haven't been harsh enough. I've always let them do exactly as they liked. I should have put my foot down and not let her get married when she was only eighteen."

She was standing up with her back to him. She turned round and said, "Hallo, Dad."

"This is a bad business, Sylvia."

Wexford loved both his daughters dearly, but Sheila, the younger, was his favourite. Sheila had the career, the tough life, had been through the hardening process but had remained soft and sweet. Also she looked like him, although he was an ugly man and everyone called her beautiful. Sylvia's hard classical features were those of his late mother-in-law, and hers the Britannia bust and majestic bearing. She had led the protected and sheltered existence in the town where she had been born. But while Sheila would have run to him and called him Pop and thrown her arms round him, this girl stood staring at him with tragic calm, one marmoreal arm extended along the mantelpiece.

"I don't suppose you want me here, Dad," she said. "I'd nowhere else to go. I won't bother you for long. I'll get a job and find somewhere for me and the boys to live."

"Don't speak to me like that, Sylvia. Please don't.

This is your home. What have I ever said to you to make you speak to me like that?"

She didn't move. Two great tears appeared in her eyes and coursed slowly down her cheeks. Her father went up to her and took her in his arms, wondering as he did so when it was that he had last held her like this. Years ago, long before she was married. At last she responded, and the hug he got was vice-like, almost breath-crushing. He let her sob and gulp into his shoulder, holding her close and murmuring to this fugitive goddess, all magnificent five feet ten of her, much the same words that he had used twenty years before when she had fallen and cut her knee.

More negative results awaited him on Monday morning. The phone calls were still coming in, growing madder as time went by. No newspaper in the country knew of Rhoda Comfrey either as an employee or in a free-lance capacity, no press agency, no magazine, and she was not on record as a member of the National Union of Journalists.

Detective Constable Loring had left for London by an early train, bound for the leather shop in Jermyn Street. Wexford wished now that he had gone himself, for he was made irritable by this enforced inactivity and by thoughts of what he had left behind him at home. Tenderness he felt for Sylvia, but little sympathy. Robin and Ben had been told their father was going away on business and that was why they were there, but although Ben accepted this, Robin perhaps knew better. He was old enough to have been affected by the preceding quarrels and to have understood much of what had been said. Without him and Ben, their mother would have been able to lead a free, worth-while and profitable life. The little boy went about with a bewildered look. That damned water rat might have provided a diversion, but the beast was as elusive as ever.

And Neil had not come. Wexford had been sure his

son-in-law would turn up, even if only for more re-
criminations and mud-slinging. He had neither come
nor phoned. And Sylvia, who had said she didn't want
him to come, that she never wanted to see him again,
first moped over his absence, then harangued her parents for allowing her to marry him in the first place.
Wexford had had a bad night because Dora had hardly
slept, and in the small hours he had heard Sylvia pacing
her bedroom or roving the house.

Loring came back at twelve, which was the earliest he
could possibly have made it, and Wexford found himself perversely wishing he had been late so that he could
have snapped at him. That was no way to go on.
Pleasantly he said,

"Did you get any joy?"

"In a sort of way, sir. They recognised the wallet at
once. It was the last of a line they had left. The customer bought it on Thursday, August fourth."

"You call that a sort of way? I call it a bloody mar-
vellous break."

Loring looked pleased, though it was doubtful
whether this was praise or even directed at him. "Not
Rhoda Comfrey, sir," he said hastily. "A man. Chap
called Grenville West. He's a regular customer of Silk
and Whitebeam. He's bought a lot of stuff from them
in the past."

"Did you get his address?"

"Twenty-two, Elm Green, London, West 15," said
Loring.

No expert on the metropolis, Wexford nevertheless
knew a good deal of the geography of the London
Borough of Kenbourne. And now, in his mind's eye, he
saw Elm Green that lay half a mile from the great
cemetery. Half an acre or so of turf with elm trees on
it, a white-painted fence bordering two sides of it, and
facing the green, a row of late-Georgian houses, some
with their ground floors converted into shops. A pretty
place, islanded in sprawling, squalid Kenbourne which,

like the curate's egg and all London Boroughs, was good in parts.

It was a piece of luck for him that this first possible London acquaintance—friend, surely—of Rhoda Comfrey had been located here. He would get help, meet with no obstruction, for his own nephew, his dead sister's son, was head of Kenbourne Vale C.I.D. That Chief Superintendent Howard Fortune was at present away on holiday in the Canary Islands was a pity but no real hindrance. Several members of Howard's team were known to him. They were old friends.

By two Stevens, his driver, was heading the car towards London. Wexford relaxed, feeling his confidence returning, Sylvia and her troubles pushed to the back of his mind, and he felt stimulated by the prospect before him when Stevens set him down outside Kenbourne Vale Police Station.

"Inspector Baker in?"

It was amusing, really. If anyone had told him, those few years before, that the day would come when he would actually be asking for Baker, wanting to see him, he would have laughed with resentful scorn. For Baker had been the reverse of pleasant to him when, convalescing after his thrombosis with Howard and Denise, he had helped solve the cemetery murder. But Howard, Wexford thought secretly, would have refused that word "helped," would have said his uncle had done all that solving on his own. And that had marked the beginning of Baker's respect and friendship. After that, there had been no more barbs about rustic policemen and interference and ignorance of London thugs.

His request was answered in the affirmative, and two minutes later he was being shown down one of those bottle-green-painted corridors to the inspector's office with its view of a brewery. Baker got up and came to him delightedly, hand outstretched.

"This is a pleasant surprise, Reg!"

It was getting on for two years since Wexford had seen him. In that time, he thought, there had been more remarkable changes, and not just in the man's manner towards himself. He looked years younger, he looked happy. Only the harsh corncrake voice with its faint cockney intonation remained the same.

"It's good to see you, Michael." Baker shared Burden's Christian name. How that had once riled him! "How are you? You're looking fine. What's the news?"

"Well, you'll know Mr. Fortune's away in Tenerife. Things are fairly quiet here, thank God. Your old friend Sergeant Clements is somewhere about, he'll be glad to see you. Sit down and I'll have some tea sent up." There was a framed photograph of a fair-haired, gentle-looking woman on the desk. Baker saw Wexford looking at it. "My wife," he said, self-conscious, proud, a little embarrassed. "I don't know if Mr. Fortune mentioned I'd got married"—a tiny hesitation "—again?"

Yes, Howard had, of course, but he had forgotten. The new ease of manner, the happiness, were explained. Michael Baker had once been married to a girl who had become pregnant by another man and who had left him for that other man. Finding that out from Howard had marked the beginnings of his toleration of Baker's rudeness and his thinly veiled insults.

"Congratulations. I'm delighted."

"Yes, well . . ." Awkwardness brought out shades of Baker's old acerbity. "You didn't come here to talk about my domestic bliss. You came about this Rose— no, Rhoda—Comfrey. Am I right?"

Wexford said on a surge of hope, "You know her? You've got some . . . ?"

"Wouldn't I have been in touch if I had? No, but I read the papers. I don't suppose you've got much else on your mind at the moment, have you?"

Sylvia, Sylvia . . . "No, not much." The tea came, and he told Baker about the wallet and Grenville West.

"I do know *him*. Well, not to say 'know.' He's what you might call our contribution to the arts. They put bits about him in the local paper from time to time.

Come on, Reg, I always think of you as so damned intellectual. Don't tell me you've never heard of Grenville West?"

"Well, I haven't. What does he do?"

"I dare say he's not that famous. He writes books, historical novels. I can't say I've ever set eyes on him, but I've read one of his books—bit above my head— and I can tell you a bit about him from what I've seen in the paper. In his late thirties, dark-haired chap, smokes a pipe—they put his photo on his book jackets. You know those old houses facing the Green? He lives in a flat in one of them over a wine bar."

Having courteously refused Baker's offer of assistance, sent his regards to Sergeant Clements, and promised to return later, he set off up Kenbourne High Street. The heat that was pleasant, acceptable, in the country, made of this London suburb a furnace that seemed to be burning smelly refuse. A greyish haze obscured the sun. He wondered why the Green looked different, barer somehow, and bigger. Then he noticed the stumps where the trees had been. So Dutch Elm Disease denuded London as well as the country.

He crossed the grass where black children and one white child were playing ball, where two Indian women in saris, their hair in long braids, walked slowly and gracefully as if they carried invisible pots on their heads. The wine bar had been discreetly designed not to mar the long elegant facade, as had the other shops in this row, and the sign over its bow window announced in dull gold letters: Vivian's Vineyard. The occasional slender tree grew out of the pavement, and some of the houses had window-boxes with geraniums and petunias in them. Across the house next door to the bar rambled the vines of an *ipomaea,* the Morning Glory, its trumpet flowers open and glowing a brilliant blue. This might have been some corner of Chelsea or Hampstead. If you kept your eyes steady, if you didn't look south to the gasworks or east to St. Bid-

dulph's Hospital, if you didn't smell the smoky, diesel-y
stench, it might even have been Kingsmarkham.

He rang repeatedly at the door beside the shop window, but no one came. Grenville West was out. What
now? It was nearly five and, according to the notice on
the shop door, the Vineyard opened at five. He sat
down on one of the benches on the Green to wait until
it did.

Presently a pale-skinned negroid girl came out,
peered up and down the street and went back in again,
turning the sign to OPEN. Wexford followed her and
found himself in a dim cavern, light coming only from
some bulbs behind the bar itself and from heavily-
shaded Chianti bottle lamps on the tables. The window
was curtained in brown and silver and the curtains were
fast drawn. On a high stool, under the most powerful
of the lamps, the pale Negress had seated herself to leaf
through a magazine.

He asked her for a glass of white wine, and then if
the owner or manager or proprietor was about.

"You want Vic?"

"I expect I do if he's the boss."

"I'll fetch him."

She came back with a man who looked in his early
forties. "Victor Vivian. What can I do for you?"

Wexford showed him his warrant card and explained. Vivian seemed rather cheered by the unex-
pected excitement, while the girl opened enormous eyes
and stared.

"Take a pew," said Vivian not ineptly, for the place
had the gloom of a chapel devoted to some esoteric
cult. But there was nothing priestly about its proprietor.
He wore jeans and a garment somewhere between a
T-shirt and a wind-cheater with a picture on it of
peasant girls treading out the grape harvest. "Gren's
away. Went off on a holiday to France, you know—let's
see now—last Sunday week. He always goes to France
for a month at this time of the year."

"You own the house?"

"Not to say 'own,' you know. I mean, Notbourne Properties own it. I've got the under-lease."

He was going to be an "I mean-er" and "you know-er." Wexford could feel it coming. Still, such people usually talked a lot and were seldom discreet. "You know him well?"

"We're old mates, Gren and me, you know. He's been here fourteen years and a damn' good tenant. I mean, he does all his repairs himself and it's handy, you know, having someone always on the premises when the bar's closed. Most evenings he'll drop in here for a drink, you know, and then as often as not I'll have a quick one with him, up in his place, I mean, after we've knocked off for the night, and then, you know . . ."

Wexford cut this useless flow short. "It's not Mr. West I'm primarily interested in. I'm trying to trace the address of someone who may have been a friend of his. You've read of the murder of Miss Rhoda Comfrey?"

Vivian gave a schoolboy whistle. "The old girl who was stabbed? You mean she was a friend of Gren's? Oh, I doubt that, I mean, I doubt that very much. I mean, she was fifty, wasn't she? Gren's not forty, I mean, I doubt if he's more than thirty-eight or thirty-nine. Younger than me, you know."

"I wasn't suggesting the relationship was a sexual one, Mr. Vivian. They could just have been friends."

This possibility was apparently beyond Vivian's comprehension, and he ignored it. "Gren's got a girl friend. Nice little thing, you know, worships the ground he treads on." A sly wink was levelled at Wexford. "He's a wily bird, though, is old Gren. Keeps her at arm's length a bit. Afraid she might get him to the altar, you know, or that's my guess, I mean. Polly something or other, she's called, blonde—I mean, she can't be more than twenty-four or -five. Came to do his typ-

ing, you know, and now she hangs on like the prover-
bial limpet. Have another drink? On the house, I
mean."

"No, thank you, I won't." Wexford produced the
photograph and the wallet. "You've never seen this
woman? She'd changed a lot, she didn't look much like
that any more, I'm afraid."

Vivian shook his head and his beard waggled. He
had a variety of intense facial contortions, all stereo-
typed and suggesting the kind a ham actor acquires to
express astonishment, sagacity, knowingness and suspicion. "I've never seen her here or with Gren, you
know," he said, switching on the one that indicated
disappointed bewilderment. "Funny, though, I mean,
there's something familiar about the face. Something,
you know, I can't put a finger on it. Maybe it'll come
back." As Wexford's hopes leapt, Vivian crushed them.
"This picture wasn't in the papers, was it? I mean,
could that be where I've seen her before?"

"It could."

Two people came into the bar, bringing with them
a momentary blaze of sunshine before the door closed
again. Vivian waved in their direction, then, turning
back, gave a low whistle. "I say! That isn't old Gren's
wallet, is it?"

Vague memories of Latin lessons came back to
Wexford, of forms in which to put questions expecting
the answer no. All Vivian's questions seemed to expect
the answer no, perhaps so that he could whistle and
put on his astounded face when he got a yes.

"Well, is it?"

"Now wait a minute. I mean, this one's new, isn't
it? You caught me out for a minute, you know. Gren's
got one like it, only a bit knocked around, I mean. Just
like that, only a bit battered. Not new, I mean."

And he had taken it with him to France, Wexford
thought. He was making slow progress, but he kept
trying. "This woman was almost certainly living under
an assumed name, Mr. Vivian. Never mind the name

or the face. Did Mr. West ever mention to you any woman friend he had who was older than himself?"

"There was his agent, his what-d'you-call-it?—literary agent. I can't remember her name. Mrs. Something, you know. Got a husband living, I'm sure of that. I mean, it wouldn't be her, would it?"

"I'm afraid not. Can you tell me Mr. West's address in France?"

"He's touring about, you know. Somewhere in the south, that's all I can tell you. Getting back to this woman, I'm racking my brains, but I can't come up with anyone. I mean, people chat to you about this and that, especially in my job, I mean, and a lot of it goes in one ear and out the other. Old Gren goes about a lot, great walker, likes his beer, likes to have a walk about Soho at night. For the pubs, I mean, nothing nasty, I don't mean that. He's got his drinking pals, you know, and he may have talked of some woman, but I wouldn't have the faintest idea about her name or where she lived, would I? I mean, I'm sorry I can't be of more help. But you know how it is, I mean, you don't think anyone's going to ask, I mean, it doesn't cross your mind, does it?"

As Wexford rose to go, he was unable to resist the temptation.

"I know what you mean," he said.

7

"You're not having much luck," said Baker over a fresh pot of tea. "I'll tell you what I'll do. I'll have someone go through the Kenbourne street directory for you. If he did know her, she might have been living only a stone's throw away."

"Not as Rhoda Comfrey. But it's very good of you, Michael."

Stevens was waiting for him, but they hadn't got far along Kenbourne High Street when Wexford noticed a large newish public library on the opposite side. It would close, he guessed, at six, and it was a quarter to now. He told Stevens to drop him and park the car as best he could in this jungle of buses and container lorries and double yellow lines, and then he got out and jay-walked in most un-policeman-like fashion across the road.

On the forecourt stood a bronze of a mid-nineteenth century gentleman in a frock coat. "Edward Edwards" said a plaque at its feet, that and no more, as if the name ought to be as familiar as Victoria R or William Ewart Gladstone. It wasn't familiar to Wexford, and he had no time to waste wondering about it.

He went on into the library and its large fiction section, and there he was, rubbing shoulders with Rebecca and Morris. Three of Grenville West's novels were in, *Killed with Kindness, The Venetian Courtesan, Fair Wind to Alicante,* and each was marked on the spine with an H for Historical. The first title appealed to him most and he took the book from the shelf and looked at the publisher's blurb on the front inside flap of the jacket.

"Once again," he read, "Mr. West astonishes us with his virtuosity in taking the plot and characters of an Elizabethan drama and clothing them in his fine rich prose. This time it is Mistress Nan Frankford, from Thomas Heywood's *A Woman Killed with Kindness,* who holds the stage. At first a loving and faithful wife, she is seduced by her husband's trusted friend, and it is her remorse and Frankford's curious generosity which contribute to the originality of this compelling book. Mr. West sticks closely to Heywood's plot, but he shows us what Heywood had no need to attempt for his contemporary audience, a vivid picture of domestic life in late sixteenth-century England with its passions, its cruelties, its conventions and its customs. A different world is unfolded before us, and we are soon aware that we are being guided through its halls, its knot gardens and its unspoilt pastoral countryside by a master of his subject."

Hmm, thought Wexford, not for him. If *Killed with Kindness* was from Heywood's play of almost identical title, *The Venetian Courtesan* was very likely based on Webster's *The White Devil* and *Fair Wind to Alicante* —on what? Wexford had a quick look at the blurb inside the jacket of that one and saw that its original was *The Changeling* of Middleton and Rowley.

A clever idea, he thought, for those who liked that sort of thing. It didn't look as if the author went in for too much intellectual stuff, but concentrated on the blood, thunder and passion which, from the point of view of his sales, was wise of him. There were a lot of Elizabethan and Jacobean plays, hundreds probably, so the possibilities of West going on till he was seventy or so seemed limitless.

Killed with Kindness had been published three years before. He turned to the back of the jacket. There Grenville West was portrayed in tweeds with a pipe in his mouth. He wore glasses and had a thick fringe of dark hair. The face wasn't very interesting but the photographer's lighting effects were masterful.

Under the picture was a biography:

"Grenville West was born in London. He has a degree in history. His varied career has led him from teaching through free-lance journalism, with short spells as a courier, barman and antique dealer, to becoming a highly successful writer of historical romance. In the twelve years since his first book, *Her Grace of Amalfi*, was published, he has delighted his readers with nine more novels of which several have been translated into French, German and Italian. His novels also appear in the United States and are regularly issued in paperback.

"*Apes in Hell* was made into a successful television

play, and *Arden's Wife* has been serialised for radio.

"Mr. West is a francophile who spends most of his holidays in France, has a French car and enjoys French cooking. He is 35 years old, lives in London and is unmarried."

On the face of it, Wexford thought, the man would appear to have little in common with Rhoda Comfrey. But then he didn't really know much about Rhoda Comfrey, did he? Maybe she too had been a francophile. Mrs. Parker had told him, that when a young woman, she had taught herself French. And there was firm evidence that she had wanted to write and had tried her hand at journalism. It was possible that West had met her at a meeting of one of those literary societies, formed by amateurs who aspire to have their work published, and who had invited him to address them. Then why keep the relationship dark? In saying that there was nothing unpleasant in West's secretiveness, Vivian had only succeeded in suggesting that there was.

The library was about to close. Wexford went out and made a face at Edward Edwards who looked superciliously back at him. Stevens was waiting for him on the pavement, and together they walked back to the car which had necessarily been parked a quarter of a mile away.

He had made a mental note of the name of West's publishers, Carlyon Brent, of London, New York and Sydney. Would they tell him anything if he called them? He had a feeling they would be cagily discreet.

"I don't see what you're hoping to get, anyway," said Burden in the morning. "He's not going to have told his publishers who he gives birthday presents to, is he?"

"I'm thinking about this girl, this Polly something or other," Wexford said. "If she does his typing in his flat, which it seems as if she does, it's likely she also answers his phone. A sort of secretary, in fact. Therefore, someone at his publishers may be in the habit of speaking to her. Or, at any rate, it's possible West will have told them her name."

Their offices were located in Russell Square. He dialled the number and was put through to someone he was told was Mr. West's editor.

"Oliver Hampton speaking." A dry cool public school voice.

He listened while Wexford went somewhat awkwardly into his explanation. The awkwardness was occasioned not by Hampton's interruptions—he didn't interrupt—but by a strong extra-aural perception, carried along fifty miles of wires, that the man at the other end was incredulous, amazed and even offended.

At last Hampton said, "I couldn't possibly give you any information of that nature about one of my authors." The information "of that nature" had merely been an address at which West could be written to or spoken to, or, failing that, the name of his typist. "Frankly, I don't know who you are. I only know who you say you are."

"In that case, Mr. Hampton, I will give you a number for you to phone my Chief Constable and check."

"I'm sorry, but I'm extremely busy. In point of fact, I have no idea where Mr. West is at this moment except that he is somewhere in the South of France. What I will do is give you the number of his agent if that would help."

Wexford said it might and noted the number down. Mrs. Brenda Nunn, of Field and Bray, Literary Agents. This would be the woman Vivian had said was middle-aged and with a husband living. She was more talkative than Hampton and less suspicious, and she satisfied herself of his *bona fides* by calling him back at Kingsmarkham Police Station.

"Well, now we've done all that," she said, "I'm afraid I really can't be much help to you. I don't have an address for Mr. West in France and I'd never heard of

Rhoda Comfrey till I read about her in the papers. I do know the name of this girl who works for him. I've spoken to her on the phone. It's—well, it's Polly Flinders."

"It's *what?*"

"I know. Now you can see why it stuck in my mind. Actually, it's Pauline Flinders—heaven knows what her parents were thinking about—but Grenville—er—Mr. West—refers to her as Polly. I've no idea where she lives."

Next Wexford phoned Baker. The search of the Electoral Register had brought to light no Comfrey in the Parliamentary Constituency of Kenbourne Vale. Would Baker do the same for him in respect of a Miss Pauline Flinders? Baker would, with pleasure. The name seemed to afford him no amusement or even interest. However, he was anxious to help, and in addition would send a man to Kenbourne Green to enquire in all the local shops and of Grenville West's neighbours.

"It's all so vague," said Dr. Crocker who came to join them for lunch at the Carousel Cafe. "Even if the Comfrey woman was going under another name in London, this girl would have recognised her from the description in the papers. The photograph, unlike as it is, would have meant something to her. She'd have been in touch, she'd have read all your appeals."

"So therefore doesn't it look as if she didn't because she has something to hide?"

"It looks to me," said Burden, "as if she just didn't know her."

Waiting to hear from Baker, Wexford tried to make some sort of reasonable pattern of it. Rhoda Comfrey who, for some unknown motive, called herself something else in London, had been a fan and admirer of Grenville West, had become his friend. Perhaps she performed certain services for him in connection with his work. She might—and Wexford was rather pleased with this notion—run a photo-copying agency. That would fit in with what Mrs. Crown had told him. Suppose she had made copies of manuscripts for West free of charge, and he, in gratitude, had given her a rather special birthday present? After all, according to old Mrs. Parker, she had become fifty years old on 5 August. In some countries, Wexford knew, the fiftieth birthday was looked on as a landmark of great significance, an anniversary worthy of particular note. He had bought the wallet on the fourth, given it to her on the fifth, left for his holiday on the seventh, and she had come down to Kingsmarkham on the eighth. None of this got him nearer finding the identity of her murderer, but that was a long way off yet, he thought gloomily.

Into the midst of these reflections the phone rang.

"We've found her," said the voice of Baker. "Or we've found where she lives. She was in the register. West Kenbourne, All Souls' Grove, number 15, Flat 1. Patel, Malina N. and Flinders, Pauline J. No number in the phone book for either of them, so I sent Dinehart round, and a woman upstairs said your Flinders usually comes in around half-four. D'you want us to see her for you? It's easily done."

"No, thanks, Michael, I'll come up."

Happiness hadn't eroded all the encrusting sourness from Baker's nature. He was still quick to sense a snub where no snub was intended, still looking always for an effusively expressed appreciation. "Suit yourself," he said gruffly. "D'you know how to find All Souls' Grove?" Implicit in his tone was the suggestion that this country bumpkin might be able to find a haystack or even a needle in one, but not a street delineated in every London guide. "Turn right out of Kenbourne Lane Tube station into Magdalen Hill, right again into Balliol Street, and it's the second on the left after Oriel Mews."

Forbearing to point out that with his rank he did

rate a car and a driver, Wexford said only, "I'm most grateful, Michael, you're very good," but he was too late.

"All in the day's work," said Baker and put the phone down hard.

Wexford had sometimes wondered why it is that a plain woman so often chooses to live with, or share a flat with, or be companioned by, a beautiful woman. Perhaps choice does not enter into it; perhaps the pressure comes from the other side, from the beautiful one whose looks are set off by the contrast, while the ill-favoured one is too shy, too humble and too accustomed to her place to resist.

In this case, the contrast was very marked. Beauty had opened the front door to him, beauty in a peacock-green sari with little gold ornaments, and on hands of a fineness and delicacy seldom seen in Western women, the width across the broadest part less than three inches, rings of gold and ivory. An exquisite small face, the skin of a smoky gold, peeped at him from a cloud of silky black hair.

"Miss Patel?"

She nodded, and nodded again rather sagely when he showed her his warrant card.

"I'd like to see Miss Flinders, please."

The flat, on the ground floor, was the usual furnished place. Big rooms divided with improvised matchwood walls, old reject furniture, girls' clutter everywhere— clothes and magazines, pinned-up posters, strings of beads hanging from a door handle, half-burnt coloured candles in saucers. The other girl, the one he had come to see, turned slowly from having been hunched over a typewriter. An ash tray beside her was piled with stubs. He found himself thinking:

> Little Polly Flinders
> Sat among the cinders,
> Warming her pretty little toes. . . .

As it happened, her feet were bare under the long cotton skirt, and they were good feet, shapely and long. Perhaps, altogether, she wouldn't have been so bad if he hadn't seen Malina Patel first. She wouldn't have been bad at all but for that awful stoop, assumed no doubt in an attempt to reduce her height, though it was less than his Sylvia's, and but for the two prominent incisors in her upper jaw. Odd, he thought, in someone of her years, child of the age of orthodontics.

She came up to him, unsmiling and wary, and Malina Patel went softly away, having not spoken a word. He plunged straight into the middle of things.

"No doubt you've read the papers, Miss Flinders, and seen about the murder of a Miss Rhoda Comfrey. This photograph was in the papers. Imagine it, if you can, aged by about twenty years and its owner using another name."

She looked at the photograph and he watched her. He could make nothing of her expression, it seemed quite blank.

"Do you think you have ever seen her? In, let us say, the company of Mr. Grenville West?"

A flush coloured her face unbecomingly. Victor Vivian had described her as a blonde, and that word is very evocative, implying beauty and a glamorous femininity, a kind of Marilyn Monroe-ishness. Pauline Flinders was not at all like that. Her fairness was just an absence of colour, the eyes a watery pale grey, the hair almost white. Her blush was vivid and patchy under that pale skin, and he supposed it was his mention of the man's name that had caused it. Not guilty knowledge, though, but love.

"I've never seen her," she said, and then, "Why do you think Grenville knew her?"

He wasn't going to answer that yet. She kept looking towards the door as if she were afraid the other girl would come back. Because her flat-mate had teased her about her feelings for the novelist?

"You're Mr. West's secretary, I believe?"

"I had an advertisement in the local paper saying I'd do typing for people. He phoned me. That was about two years ago. I did a manuscript for him and he liked it and I started sort of working for him part-time." She had a graceless way of speaking, in a low dull monotone.

"So you answered his phone, no doubt, and met his friends. Was there anyone among his friends who might possibly have been this woman?"

"Oh, no, no one." She sounded certain beyond a doubt, and she added fatuously, with a lover's obsessiveness, "Grenville's in France. I had a card from him." Why wasn't it on the mantelpiece? As she slipped the postcard out from under a pile of papers beside her typewriter, Wexford thought he knew the answer to that one too. She didn't want to be teased about it.

A coloured picture of Annecy, and "Annecy" was clearly discernible on the otherwise smudged postmark. "Greetings from France, little Polly Flinders, the sunshine, the food, the air and the *bel aujourd'hui*. I shan't want to come back. But I shall— So, see you. G.W." Typical of one of those literary blokes, he thought, but not, surely, the communication of a lover. Why had she shown it to him with its mention of her whimsical nickname? Because it was all she had?

He brought out the wallet and laid it down beside the postcard. What he wanted was for her to shriek, turn pale, cry out, "Where did you get that?"—demolish the structure of ignorance he fancied she might carefully have built up. She did nothing but stare at it with the same guarded expression.

"Have you ever seen this before, Miss Flinders?"

She looked at it inside and out. "It looks like Grenville's wallet," she said, "the one he lost."

"Lost?" said Wexford.

She seemed to gain self-confidence and her voice some animation. "He was coming back from the West End on a bus, and when he came in he said he'd left his wallet on the bus. That must have been Thursday or Friday week. Where did you find it?"

"In Miss Rhoda Comfrey's handbag." He spoke slowly and heavily. So that was the answer. No connection, no relationship between author and admiring fan, no fiftieth birthday present. She had found it on a bus and kept it. "Did Mr. West report his loss?"

When she was silent she tried to cover her protruding teeth, as people with this defect do, by pushing her lower lip out over them. Now the teeth appeared again. They caused her to lisp a little. "He asked me to, but I didn't. I didn't exactly forget. But someone told me the police don't really like you reporting things you've lost or found. A policeman my mother knows told her it makes too much paper work."

He believed her. Who knew better than he that the police are not angels in uniform, sacrificing themselves to the public good? Leaving her to return to her typewriter, he went out into the big gloomy hall of the house. The flat door opened again behind him and Malina Patel appeared with a flash bright as a kingfisher. Her accent, as English and as prettily correct as his Sheila's, surprised him nearly as much as what she said.

"Polly was here with me all the evening on the eighth. She was helping me make a dress, she was cutting it out." Her smile was mischievous and her teeth perfect. "You're a detective, aren't you?"

"That's right."

"What a freaky thing to be. I've never seen one before except on the T.V." She spoke as if he were some rare animal, an eland perhaps. "Do people give you a lot of money? Like 'Fifty thousand dollars to find my daughter, she's all the world to me'—that kind of thing?"

"I'm afraid not, Miss Patel."

He could have sworn she was mocking her friend's dull naivety. The lovely face became guileless, the eyes opened hugely.

"When you first came to the door," she said, "I thought you might be a bailiff. We had one of those before when we hadn't paid the rates."

8

A red-hot evening in Kenbourne Vale, a dusty dying sun. The reek of cumin came to him from Kemal's Kebab House, beer and sweat from the Waterlily pub. All the eating and drinking places had their doors wide open, propped back. Children of all ages, all colors, pure races and mixed races, sat on flights of steps or rode two- and three-wheelers on hard pavements and up and down narrow stuffy alleys. An old woman, drunk or just old and sick, squatted in the entrance to a betting shop. There was nothing green and organic to be seen unless you counted the lettuces, stuffed tight into boxes outside a greengrocer's, and they looked as much like plastic as their wrappings.

One thing to be thankful for was that now he need not come back to Kenbourne Vale ever again if he didn't want to. The trail had gone cold, about the only thing that had this evening. Sitting in the car on the road back to Kingsmarkham, he thought about it. At first Malina Patel's behaviour had puzzled him. Why had she come out voluntarily to provide herself or Polly Flinders with an unasked-for alibi? Because she was a tease and a humourist, he now reflected, and in her beauty dwelt with wit. Everything she had said to him had been calculated to amuse—and how she herself had smiled at the time!—all that about telly detectives and bailiffs. Very funny and charming from such a pretty girl. But no wonder Polly kept the postcard hidden and feared her overhearing their conversation. He could imagine the Indian girl's comments.

But if she hadn't been listening at the door how the hell had she known what he had come for? Easy. The woman upstairs had told her. One of Baker's men—that none too reliable Dinehart probably—had been round earlier in the day and let slip not only that the Kingsmarkham Police wanted to talk to Polly but why they had wanted to talk to her. Malina would have read the papers, noted the date of Rhoda Comfrey's death. He remembered how closely and somehow complacently she had looked at his warrant card. Rather a naughty girl she was, playing detective stories and trying to throw cats among pigeons to perplex him and tease her flatmate.

Ah, well, it was over now. Rhoda Comfrey had found that wallet on a bus or in the street, and he was back where he started.

Just before nine he walked into his own house. Dora was out, as he had known she would be, baby-sitting for Burden's sister-in-law, Sylvia nowhere to be seen or heard. In the middle of the staircase sat Robin in pyjamas.

"It's too hot to go to sleep. You aren't tired, are you, Grandad?"

"Not really," said Wexford who was.

"Granny said you would be but I know you, don't I? I said to Granny that you'd want some fresh air."

"River air? Put some clothes on, then, and tell Mummy where you're going."

Twilight had come to the water meadows. "Dusk is a very good time for water rats," said Robin. "Dusk." He seemed to like the word and repeated it over and over as they walked along the river bank. Above the sluggish flow of the Kingsbrook gnats danced in lazy clouds. But the heat was not oppressive, the air was sweet and a refreshment to a London-jaded spirit.

However, "I'm afraid we've had it for tonight," Wexford said as the darkness began to deepen.

Robin took his hand. "Yes, we'd better go back because my daddy's coming. I thought he was in Sweden, but he's not. I expect we'll go home tomorrow. Not tonight because Ben's asleep."

Wexford didn't know what answer to make. And when they came into the hall he heard from behind the closed door of the living room the angry but lowered voices of his daughter and son-in-law. Robin made no move towards that door. He looked at it, looked away, and rubbed his fists across his tired eyes.

"I'll see you into bed," said his grandfather and lifted him more than usually tenderly in his arms.

In the morning they phoned him from Stowerton Royal Infirmary. They thought the police would wish to know that Mr. James Comfrey had "passed away" during the night, and since his daughter was dead, whom should they get in touch with?

"Mrs. Lilian Crown," he said, and then he thought he might as well go and see her himself. There was little else to do.

She was out. In Kingsmarkham the pubs open at ten on market day. To Bella Vista then. Today its name, its viridian roof and its sun-trap windows were justified. Light and heat beat down with equal force from a sky of the same hard dark blue as the late Mr. Comfrey's front door.

"He's gone then," the old woman said. News travels fast in these quiet backwoods places. During the hour that had passed since Wexford had been told the news, Mrs. Crown also had been told and had informed at least some of her neighbours. "It's a terrible thing to die, young man, and have no one shed a tear for you."

She was stringing beans today, slicing them into long thin strips as few young housewives can be bothered to do. "I dare say it'd have been a relief to poor Rhoda. Whatever'd she have done, I used to ask myself, if they'd turned him out of there and she'd had to look after him? Nursed her mother devotedly, she did, used to have to take time off work and all, but there was love there of course, and not a word of appreciation from old Jim." The vital youthful eyes fixed piercingly on him. "Who'll get the money?"

"The money, Mrs. Parker?"

"Rhoda's money. It'd have gone to him, being next of kin. I know that. Who'll get it now? That's what I'd like to know."

This aspect hadn't occurred to him. "Maybe there isn't any money. Few working people these days have much in the way of savings."

"Speak up, will you?"

Wexford repeated what he had said, and Mrs. Parker gave a scornful cackle.

"Course there's money. She got that lot from her pools win, didn't she? Wouldn't have blowed that, not Rhoda, she wasn't one of your spendthrifts. I reckon you lot have been sitting about twiddling your thumbs or you'd have got to the bottom of it by now. A house there'll be somewhere, filled up with good furniture, and a nice little sum in shares too. D'you want to know what I think? It'll all go to Lilian Crown."

Rather unwillingly he considered what she had said. But would it go to Mrs. Crown? Possibly, but for that intervening heir, James Comfrey. If she had had anything to leave and if she had died intestate, James Comfrey had for nine days been in possession of his daughter's property. But a sister-in-law wouldn't automatically inherit from him, though her son, the mongol, if he were still alive . . . A nephew by marriage? He knew little of the law relating to inheritance, and it hardly seemed relevant now.

"Mrs. Parker," he said, pitching his voice loud, "you're quite right when you say we haven't got very far. But we do know Miss Comfrey was living under an assumed name, a false name. Do you follow me?" She nodded impatiently. "Now when people do that, they often choose a name that's familiar to them, a mother's maiden name, for instance, or the name of some relative or childhood friend."

"Whyever would she do that?"

"Perhaps only because her own name had very unpleasant associations for her. Do you know what her mother's maiden name was?"

Mrs. Parker had it ready. "Crawford. Agnes and Lilian Crawford, they was. Change the name and not the letter, change for worse and not for better. Poor Agnes changed for worse all right, and the same applies to that Lilian, though it wasn't a C for her the first time. Crown left her and he's got another wife somewhere, I dare say, for all she says he's dead."

"So she might have been calling herself Crawford?" he was speaking his thoughts aloud. "Or Parker, since she was so fond of you. Or Rowlands after the editor of the old *Gazette.*" This spoken reverie had scarcely been audible to Mrs. Parker, and he bawled out his last suggestion. "Or Crown?"

"Not Crown. She hadn't no time for that Lilian. And no wonder, always mocking her and telling her to get herself a man." The old face contorted and Mrs. Parker put up her fists as the aged do, recalling that far-distant childhood when such a gesture was natural. "Why'd she call herself anything but her rightful name? She was a good woman was Rhoda, never did anything wrong nor underhand in her whole life."

Could you truthfully say that of anyone? Not, certainly, of Rhoda Comfrey who had stolen something she must have known would be precious to its owner, and whose whole life could be described as a masterpiece of underhandedness.

"I'll go out this way, Mrs. Parker," he said, opening the french window to the garden because he didn't want to encounter Nicky.

"Mind you shut it behind you. They can talk about heat all they like, but my hands and feet are always cold like yours'll be, young man, when you get to my age."

There was no sign of Mrs. Crown. He hadn't checked her movements on the night in question, but was it within the bounds of possibility that she had killed her niece? The motive was very tenuous, unless she knew of the existence of a will. Certainly there might be a will, deposited with a firm of solicitors who were unaware of the testator's death, but Rhoda Comfrey would never have left anything to the aunt she so disliked. Besides, that little stick of a woman wouldn't have had the physical strength . . .

His car, its windows closed and its doors locked for safety's sake, was oven-hot inside, the steering wheel almost too hot to hold. Driving back, he was glad he was a thin man now so that at least the trickling sweat didn't make him look like a pork carcase in the preliminary stages of roasting.

Before the sun came round, he closed the windows in his office and pulled down the blinds. Somewhere or other he had read that that was what they did in hot countries rather than let the air in. Up to a point it worked. Apart from a short break for lunch in the canteen, he sat up there for the rest of the day, thinking, thinking. He couldn't remember any previous case that had come his way in which, after nine days, he had had no possible suspect, could see no glimmer of a motive, or knew less about the victim's private life. Hours of thinking got him no further than to conclude that the killing had been, wildly incongruous though it seemed, a crime of passion, that it had been unpremeditated, and that Mrs. Parker had allowed affection to sway her assessment of Rhoda Comfrey's character.

"Where's your mother?" said Wexford, finding his daughter alone.

"Upstairs, reading bedtime stories."

"Sylvia," he said, "I've been busy, I'm still very

busy, but I hope there'll never be a time when I've got too much on my hands to think about my children. Is there anything I can do to help? When I'm not being a policeman that's what I'm here for."

She hung her head. Large and statuesque, she had a face designed, it seemed, to register the noble virtues of courage and fortitude. She was patience on a monument, smiling at grief. Yet she had never known grief, and in her life hardly any courage or fortitude had ever been called for.

"Wouldn't you like to talk about it?" he said.

The strong shoulders lifted. "We can't change the facts. I'm a woman and that's to be a second-rate citizen."

"You didn't use to feel like this."

"Oh, Dad, what's the use of talking like that? People change. We don't hold the same opinions all our lives. If I say I read a lot of books and went to some meetings, you'll only say what Neil says, that I shouldn't have read them and I shouldn't have gone."

"Maybe I shall and maybe I'd be right if what you've read has turned you from a happy woman into an unhappy one and is breaking up your marriage. Are you less of a second-rate citizen here with your parents than at home with your husband?"

"I shall be if I get a job, if I start training for something now."

Her father forebore to tell her that he hardly cared for the idea of her attending some college or course while her mother was left to care for Robin and Ben. Instead he asked her if she didn't think that to be a woman had certain advantages. "If you get a flat tyre," he said, "the chances are in five minutes some chap'll stop and change the wheel for you for no more reason than that you've got a good figure and a nice smile. But if it was me I could stand there flagging them down for twenty-four hours without a hope in hell of even getting the loan of a jack."

"Because I'm pretty!" she said fiercely, and he almost laughed, the adjective was so inept. Her eyes flashed, she looked like a Medea. "D'you know what that means? Whistles, yes, but no respect. Stupid compliments but never a sensible remark as from one human being to another."

"Come now, you're exaggerating."

"I am not, Dad. Look, I'll give you an example. A couple of weeks ago Neil backed the car into the gatepost and I took it to the garage to get a new rear bumper and light. When the mechanics had done whistling at me, d'you know what the manager said? 'You ladies,' he said, 'I bet he had a thing or two to say when he saw what you'd done.' *He took it for granted* I'd done it because I'm a woman. And when I corrected him he couldn't talk seriously about it. Just flirtatiousness and silly cracks and I was to explain this and that to Neil. 'His motor', he said, and to tell *him* this, that and the other. I know as much about cars as Neil. It's as much my car as his." She stopped and flushed. "No, it isn't, though!" she burst out. "It isn't! And it isn't as much my house as his. My children aren't even as much mine as his, he's their legal guardian. My God, my life isn't as much mine as his!"

"I think we'd better have a drink," said her father, "and you calm down a bit and tell me just what your grievances against Neil are. Who knows? I may be able to be your intermediary."

Thus he found himself, a couple of hours later, closeted with his son-in-law in the house which he had, in former times, delighted to visit because it was noisy and warm and filled, it had seemed to him, with love. Now it was dusty, chilly and silent. Neil said he had had his dinner but, from the evidence, Wexford thought it had taken a liquid and spirituous form.

"Of course I want her back, Reg, and my kids. I love her, you know that. But I can't meet her conditions. I won't. I'm to have some wretched *au pair* here which'll mean the boys moving in together, pay her a salary I can ill afford, just so that Syl can go off and train for some profession that's already overcrowded. She's a damn good wife and mother, or she was. I don't see any reason to employ someone to do the things she does so well while she trains for something she may not do well at all. Have a drink?"

"No, thanks."

"Well, I will, and you needn't tell me I've had too much already. I know it. The point is, why can't she go on doing her job while I do mine? I don't say hers is less important than mine. I don't say she's inferior, and when she says others say so I think that's all in her head. But I'm not paying her a wage for doing what other women have done since time immemorial for love. Right? I'm not going to jeopardise my career by cancelling trips abroad, or exhaust myself cleaning the place and bathing the kids when I get home after a long day. I'll dry the dishes, O.K., I'll see she gets any labour-saving equipment she wants, but I'd like to know just who needs the liberation if I'm to work all day and all night while she footles around at some college for God knows how many years. I wish I was a woman, I can tell you, no money worries, no real responsibility, no slogging off to an office day in and day out for forty years."

"You don't wish that, you know."

"I almost have done this week." Neil threw out a despairing hand at the chaos surrounding him. "I don't know how to do housework, I can't cook, but I can earn a decent living. Why the hell can't she do the one and I do the other like we used to? I could wring those damned Women's Libbers' necks. I love her, Reg. There's never been anyone else for either of us. We row, of course we do, that's healthy in a marriage, but we love each other and we've got two super kids. Doesn't it seem crazy that a sort of political thing, an impersonal thing, could split up two people like us?"

"It's not impersonal to her," said Wexford sadly. "Couldn't you compromise, Neil? Couldn't you get a woman in just for a year till Ben goes to school?"

"Couldn't she wait just for a year till Ben goes to school? O.K., so marriage is supposed to be give and take. It seems to me I do all the giving and she does all the taking."

"And she says it's the other way about. I'll go now, Neil." Wexford laid his hand on his son-in-law's arm. "Don't drink too much. It's not the answer."

"Isn't it? Sorry, Reg, but I've every intention tonight of getting smashed out of my mind."

Wexford said nothing to his daughter when he got home, and she asked him no questions. She was sitting by the still-open french window, cuddling close to her Ben who had awakened and cried, and reading with mutinous concentration a book called *Woman and the Sexist Plot*.

9

Ben passed a fractious night and awoke at seven with a sore throat. Sylvia and her mother were discussing whether to send for Dr. Crocker or take Ben to the surgery when Wexford had to leave for work. The last thing he expected was that he himself would be spending the morning in a doctor's surgery, for he saw the day ahead as a repetition of the day before, to be passed in fretful inertia behind drawn blinds.

He was a little late getting in. Burden was waiting for him, impatiently pacing the office.

"We've had some luck. A doctor's just phoned in. He's got a practice in London, and he says Rhoda Comfrey was on his list, she was one of his patients."

"My God. At last. Why didn't he call us sooner?"

"Like so many of them, he was away on holiday. In the South of France, oddly enough. Didn't know a thing about it till he got back last night and saw one of last week's newspapers."

"I suppose you said we'd want to see him?"

Burden nodded. "He expects to have seen the last of his surgery patients by eleven and he'll wait in for us. I said I thought we could be there soon after that." He referred to the notes he had taken. "He's a Dr. Christopher Lomond and he's in practice at a place called Midsomer Road, Parish Oak, London, W.19."

"Never heard of it," said Wexford. "But come to that, I've only just about heard of Stroud Green and Nunhead and Earlsfield. All those lost villages swallowed up in . . . what are you grinning at?"

"I know where it is. I looked it up. It may be W.19, but it's still part of your favourite beauty spot, the London Borough of Kenbourne."

"Back again," said Wexford. "I might have known it. And what's more, Stevens has gone down with the flu—flu in August!—so unless you feel like playing dodgem cars, it's train for us."

Though unlikely to be anyone's favourite beauty spot, the district in which they found themselves was undoubtedly the best part of Kenbourne. It lay some couple of miles to the north of Elm Green and Kenbourne High Street and the library, and it was one of those "nice" suburbs which sprang up to cover open country between the two world wars. The tube station was called Parish Oak, and from there they were directed to catch a bus which took them up a long hilly avenue, flanked by substantial houses whose front gardens had been docked for road-widening. Directly from it, at the top, debouched Midsomer Road, a street of comfortable-looking semi-detached houses, not unlike Wexford's own, where cars were tucked away into garages, doorsteps held neat little plastic containers for milk bottles, and dogs were confined behind wrought-iron gates.

Dr. Lomond's surgery was in a flat-roofed annex attached to the side of number 61. They were shown in immediately by a receptionist, and the doctor was waiting for them, a short youngish man with a cheerful pink face.

"I didn't recognise Miss Comfrey from that newspaper photograph," he said, "but I thought I remembered the name, and when I looked at the photo again I saw a sort of resemblance. So I checked with my records. Rhoda Agnes Comfrey, 6 Princevale Road, Parish Oak."

"So she hadn't often come to you, Doctor?" said Wexford.

"Only came to me once. That was last September. It's often the way, you know. They don't bother to register with a doctor till they think they've got something wrong with them. She had herself put on my list and she came straight in."

Burden said tentatively, "Would you object to telling us what was wrong with her?"

The doctor laughed breezily. "I don't think so. The poor woman's dead, after all. She thought she'd got appendicitis because she'd got pains on the right side of the abdomen. I examined her, but she didn't react to the tests and she hadn't any other symptoms, so I thought it was more likely to be indigestion and I told her to keep off alcohol and fried foods. If it persisted she was to come back and I'd give her a letter to the hospital. But she was very much against the idea of the hospital, and I wasn't surprised when she didn't come back. Look, I've got a sort of dossier thing here on her. I have one for all my patients."

He read from a card: " 'Rhoda Agnes Comfrey. Age 49. No history of disease, apart from usual childhood ailments. No surgery. Smoker—' I told her to give that up, by the way. 'Social drinker—' That can mean anything. 'Formerly registered with Dr. Castle of Glebe Road, Kingsmarkham, Sussex.' "

"And he died last year," said Wexford. "You've been a great help, Doctor. Can I trouble you to tell a stranger in these parts where Princevale Road might be?"

"Half-way down that hill you came up from the station. It turns off on the same side as this just above the block of shops."

Wexford and Burden walked slowly back to the avenue which they now noted was called Montfort Hill.

"Funny, isn't it?" said Wexford. "We know everyone else must have known her under an assumed name, but not her doctor. I wonder why not."

"Too risky?"

"What's the risk? In English law one can call oneself what one likes. What you call yourself *is* your name. People think you have to change your name by deed poll, but you don't. I could call myself Waterford tomorrow and you could call yourself Fardel without infringing a hairsbreadth of the law."

Looking puzzled, Burden said, "I suppose so. Look, I see the Waterford thing, but why Fardel?"

"You grunt and sweat under a weary life, don't you? Never mind, forget it. We won't go to Princevale Road immediately. First I want to introduce you to some friends of mine."

Baker seemed to have forgotten his cause for offence and greeted Wexford cordially.

"Michael Baker, meet Mike Burden, and this, Mike, is Sergeant Clements."

Once, though not for more than a few hours, Wexford had suspected the rubicund baby-faced sergeant of murder to be certain of the undisputed guardianship of his adopted son. It always made him feel a little guilty to remember that, even though that suspicion had never been spoken aloud. But the memory—how could he have entertained such ideas about this pillar of integrity?—had made him careful, in every subsequent conversation, to show kindness to Clements and not fail to ask after young James and the small sister chosen for him. However, the sergeant was too conscious of his subordinate rank to raise domestic matters now, and Wexford was glad of it for other reasons. He, in his turn, would have been asked for an account of his grandsons, at present a sore and embarrassing subject.

"Princevale Road?" said Baker. "Very pleasant district. Unless I'm much mistaken, number six is one of a block of what they call town houses, modern sort of places with a lot of glass and weatherboarding."

"Excuse me, sir," Clements said eagerly, "but unless *I'm* much mistaken we were called to a break-in down there a few months back. I'll nip downstairs and do a bit of checking."

Baker seemed pleased to have guests and something to relieve the tedium of August in Kenbourne Vale. "How about a spot of lunch at the Grand Duke, Reg? And then we could all get along there, if you've no objection."

Anxious to do nothing which might upset the prickly Baker, who was a man of whom it might be said that one should not touch his ears, Wexford said that he and Burden would be most gratified, adding to Baker's evident satisfaction, that he didn't know how they would get on without his help.

The sergeant came back, puffed up with news.

"The occupant is a Mrs. Farriner," he said. "She's away on holiday. It wasn't her place that was broken into, it was next door but one, but apparently she's got a lot of valuable stuff and she came in here before she went away last Saturday week to ask us to keep an eye on the house for her."

"Should put it on safe deposit," Baker began to grumble. "What's the use of getting us to. . . ."

Wexford interrupted him. He couldn't help himself. "How old is she, Sergeant? What does she look like?"

"I've not seen her myself, sir. Middle-aged, I believe, and a widow or maybe divorced. Dinehart knows her."

"Then get Dinehart to look at that photo, will you?"

"You don't mean you think Mrs. Farriner could be that Comfrey woman, sir?"

"Why not?" said Wexford.

But Dinehart was unable to say one way or another. Certainly Mrs. Farriner was a big, tall woman with dark hair who lived alone. As to her looking like that girl in the picture—well, people change a lot in twenty years. He wouldn't like to commit himself.

Wexford was tense with excitement. Why hadn't he thought of that before? All the time he was frustrated or crossed by people being away on holiday, and yet he had never considered that Rhoda Comfrey might not have been missed by friends and neighbours because they *expected* her to be absent from her home. They supposed a Mrs. Farriner to be at some resort, going under the name by which they knew her, so why connect her with a Miss Comfrey who had been found murdered in a Sussex town?

In the Grand Duke, an old-fashioned pub that had surely once been a country inn, they served themselves from the cold table. Wexford felt too keyed-up to eat much. Dealing diplomatically with people like Baker might be a social obligation, but it involved wasting a great deal of time. The others seemed to be taking what he saw as a major breakthrough far more placidly than he could. Even Burden showed a marked lack of enthusiasm.

"Doesn't it strike you as odd," he said, "that a woman like this Mrs. Farriner, well-off enough to live where she lives and have all that valuable stuff, should keep a wallet she presumably found on a bus?"

"There's nowt so strange as folk," said Wexford.

"Maybe, but it was you told me that any departure from the norm is important. I can imagine the Rhoda Comfrey *we* know doing it, but not this Mrs. Farriner from what we know of her. Therefore, it seems unlikely to me that they're one and the same."

"Well, we're not going to find out by sitting here feeding our faces," said Wexford crossly.

To his astonishment, Baker agreed with him. "You're quite right. Drink up, then, and we'll get going."

Ascending Montfort Hill on the bus, Wexford hadn't noticed the little row of five or six shops on the left-hand side. This time, in the car, his attention was only drawn to them by the fact of Burden giving them such an intense scrutiny. But he said nothing. At the moment he felt rather riled with Burden. The name of the street which turned off immediately beyond these shops was lettered in black on a white board, Princevale Road, W.19, and Burden eyed this with similar interest, craning his neck to look back when they had passed it.

At the very end of the street—or perhaps, from the numbering, the very beginning—stood a row of six terraced houses. They looked less than ten years old and differed completely in style from the detached mock-Tudor, each with a generous front garden, that characterised Princevale Road. Wexford supposed that they had been built on ground left vacant after the demolition of some isolated old house. They were a sign of the times, of scarcity of land and builders' greed. But they were handsome enough for all that, three floors high, boarded in red cedar between the wide plate-glass windows. Each had its own garage, integrated and occupying part of the ground floor, each having a different coloured front door, orange, olive, blue, chocolate, yellow and lime. Number six, at this end of the block, had the typical invitation-to-burglars look a house takes on when its affluent and prideful owner is away. All the windows were shut, all the curtains drawn back with perfect symmetry. An empty milk bottle rack stood on the doorstep, and there were no bottles, full or empty, beside it. Stuck through the letterbox and protruding from it were a fistful of letters and circulars in brown envelopes. So much for police surveillance, Wexford thought to himself.

It was rather unwillingly that he now relinquished a share of the investigating to Baker and Clements, though he knew Baker's efficiency. The hard-faced inspector and his sergeant went off to ring at the door of number one. With Burden beside him, Wexford approached the house next door to the empty one.

Mrs. Cohen at number five was a handsome Jewess in her early forties. Her house was stuffed with ornaments, the wallpaper flocked crimson on gold, gold on cream. There were photographs about of nearly grown-up children, a buxom daughter in a bridesmaid's dress, a son at his bar mitzvah.

"Mrs. Farriner's a very charming nice person. What I call a brave woman, self-supporting, you know. Yes, she's divorced. Some no-good husband in the background, I believe, though she's never told me the details and I wouldn't ask. She's got a lovely little boutique down at Montfort Circus. I've had some really exquisite things from her, and she's let me have them at cost. That's what I call neighbourly. Oh, no, it couldn't be"—looking at the photograph, "—not *murdered*. Not a false name, that's not Rose's nature. Rose Farriner, that's her name. I mean, it's laughable what you're saying. Of course I know where she is. First she went off to see her mother who's in a very nice nursing home somewhere in the country, and then she was going on to the Lake District. No, I haven't had a card from her, I wouldn't expect it."

The next house was the one which had been burgled, and Mrs. Elliott, when they had explained who they were, promptly assumed that there had been another break-in. She was at least sixty, a jumpy nervous woman who had never been in Rose Farriner's house or entertained her in her own. But she knew of the existence of the dress shop, knew that Mrs. Farriner was away and had remarked that she sometimes went away for weekends, in her view a dangerous proceeding with so many thieves about. The photograph was shown to her and she became intensely frightened. No, she couldn't say if Mrs. Farriner had looked like that when young. It was evident that the idea of even hazarding an identification terrified her, and it seemed as if by so doing she feared to put her own life in jeopardy.

"Rhoda," said Wexford to Burden, "means a rose. It's Greek for rose. She tells people she's going to visit her mother in a nursing home. What are the chances she's shifted the facts, and mother is father and the nursing home's a hospital?"

Baker and Clements met them outside the gate of number three. They too had been told of mother and the nursing home, of the dress shop, and they too had met only with doubt and bewilderment over the photograph. Together the four of them approached the last, the chocolate-coloured front door.

Mrs. Delano was very young, a fragile pallid blonde with a pale blond baby, at present asleep in its pram in the porch.

"Rose Farriner's somewhere around forty or fifty," she said, as if one of those ages was much the same as the other and all the same to her. She looked closely at the photograph, turned even paler. "I saw the papers, it never crossed my mind. It could be her. I can't imagine now why I didn't see it before."

In the display window on the left side of the shop door was the trendy gear for the very young: denim jeans and waistcoats, T-shirts, long striped socks. The other window interested Wexford more, for the clothes on show in it belonged in much the same category as those worn by Rhoda Comfrey when she met her death. Red, white and navy were the predominating colours. The dresses and coats were aimed at a comfortably-off middle-aged market. They were "smart"—

a word he knew would never be used by his daughters or by anyone under forty-five. And among them, trailing from an open sleeve to a scent bottle, suspended from a vase to the neck of a crimson sweater, were strings of glass beads.

A woman of about thirty came up to attend to them. She said her name was Mrs. Moss and she was in charge while Rose Farriner was away. Her manner was astonished, suspicious, cautious—all to be expected in the circumstances. Again the photograph was studied and again doubt was expressed. She had worked for Mrs. Farriner for only six months and knew her only in her business capacity.

"Do you know what part of the country Mrs. Farriner originally came from?" Burden asked her.

"Mrs. Farriner's never discussed private things with me."

"Would you say she's a secretive person?"

Mrs. Moss tossed her head. "I really don't know. We aren't always gossiping to each other, if that's what you mean. She doesn't know any more about me than I know about her."

Wexford said suddenly, "Has she ever had appendicitis?"

"Has she *what?*"

"Has she had her appendix out? It's the kind of thing one often does know about people."

Mrs. Moss looked as if she were about to retort that she really couldn't say, but something in Wexford's serious and ponderous gaze seemed to inhibit her. "I oughtn't to tell you things like that. It's a breach of confidence."

"You're aware as to whom we think Mrs. Farriner really is or was. I think you're being obstructive."

"But she can't be that woman. She's in the Lake District. She'll be back in the shop on Monday."

"Will she? Have you had a card from her? A phone call?"

"Of course I haven't. Why should I? I know she's coming home on Saturday."

"I'll be as frank with you," Wexford said, "as I hope you'll be with me. If Mrs. Rose Farriner has had her appendix removed she cannot be Miss Rhoda Comfrey. There was no scar from an appendectomy on Miss Comfrey's body. On the other hand, if she has not, the chances of her having been Miss Comfrey are very strong. We have to know."

"All right," said Mrs. Moss, "I'll tell you. It must have been about six months ago, about February or March. Mrs. Farriner took a few days off work. It was food poisoning, but when she came back she did say she'd thought at first it was a grumbling appendix because—well, because she'd had trouble like that before."

10

The heat danced in waving mirages on the white roadway. Traffic kept up a ceaseless swirl round Montfort Circus, and there was headache-provoking noise, a blinding glare from sunlight flashing off chrome and glass. Wexford and Baker took refuge in the car which Clements had imperiously parked on a double yellow band.

"We'll have to get into that house, Michael."

Baker said thoughtfully, "Of course, we do have a key . . ." His eye caught Wexford's. He looked away. "No, that's out of the question. It'll have to be done on a warrant. Leave it to me, Reg, I'll see what can be done."

Burden and Clements stood out on the pavement, deep in conversation. Well aware of Burden's prudishness and also of Clements' deep-rooted disapproval of pretty well all persons under twenty-five—which augured ill for James and Angela in the future—Wexford had nevertheless supposed that they would have little in common. He had been wrong. They were discussing, like old duennas, the indecent appearance of the young housewife who had opened the door of number two Princevale Road dressed only in a bikini. Wexford gave the inspector a discourteous and peremptory tap on the shoulder.

"Come on, John Knox. I want to catch the four thirty-five back to Sussex, home and beauty."

Burden looked injured, and when they had said good-bye and were crossing the Circus to Parish Oak station, remarked that Clements was a very nice chap.

"Very true," sneered Wexford with Miss Austen, "and this is a very nice day and we are taking a very nice walk."

Having no notion of what he meant but suspecting he was being got at, Burden ignored this and said they would never get a warrant on that evidence.

"What d'you mean, on that evidence? To my mind, it's conclusive. You didn't expect one of those women to come out with the whole story, did you? 'Oh, yes, Rose told me in confidence her real name's Comfrey'. Look at the facts. A woman of fifty goes to a doctor with what she thinks may be appendicitis. She gives the name of Comfrey and her address as 6 Princevale Road, Parish Oak. The only occupant of that house is a woman of around fifty called Rose Farriner. Six months later Rose Farriner is again talking of a possible appendicitis. Rhoda Comfrey is dead, Rose Farriner has disappeared. Rhoda Comfrey was comfortably off, probably had her own business. According to Mrs. Parker, she was interested in dress. Rose Farriner is well-off, has her own dress shop. Rose Farriner has a sick old mother living in a nursing home in the country. Rhoda Comfrey had a sick old father in a hospital in the country. Isn't that conclusive?"

Burden walked up and down the platform, looking gloomily at posters for pale blue movies. "I don't know. I just think we'll have trouble getting a warrant."

"There's something else bothering you, isn't there?"

"Yes, there is. It's a way-out thing. Look, it's the sort of thing that usually troubles you, not me. It's the sort of thing I usually scoff at, to tell you the truth."

"Well, what the hell is it? You might as well tell me."

Burden banged the palm of his hand with his fist. His expression was that of a man who, sceptical, practical, down-to-earth, hesitates from a fear of being laughed at to confess that he has seen a ghost. "It was when we were driving up Montfort Hill and we passed those shops, and I thought it hadn't really been worth getting a bus up that first time, it not being so far from the station to the doctor's place. And then I sort of noticed the shops and the name of the street facing us and . . . Look, it's stupid. Forget it. Frankly, the more I think about it the more I can see I was just reading something into nothing. Forget it."

"Forget it? After all that build-up? Are you crazy?"

"I'm sorry, sir," said Burden very stiffly, "but I don't approve of police work being based on silly conjectures and the sort of rubbish women call intuition. As you say, we have some very firm and conclusive facts to go on. No doubt, I was being unduly pessimistic about that warrant. Of course we'll get one."

An explosion of wrath rose in Wexford with a fresh eruption of sweat. "You're a real pain in the arse," he snapped, but the rattle of the incoming train drowned his words.

His temper was not improved by Friday morning's newspaper. POLICE CHIEF FLUMMOXED BY COMFREY CASE said a headline running across four columns at the foot of page one. And there, amid the text, was a photograph of himself, the block for which they had presumably had on file since the days when he had been a fat man. Piggy features glowered above three chins. He glowered at himself in the bathroom mirror and, thanks to Robin running in and out and shouting that grandad had got his picture in the paper, cut himself shaving the chicken skin where the three chins had used to be.

He drove to Forest Road and let himself into the late James Comfrey's house with Rhoda Comfrey's key. There were two other keys on the ring, and one of them, he was almost sure, would open Rose Farriner's front door. At the moment, though, he was keeping that to himself for comparison with the one in the possession of Kenbourne Police only if the obtaining of the warrant were held up. For if they weren't identical —and, in the light of Rhoda Comfrey's extreme secrecy about her country life in town and her town life in the country, it was likely enough they wouldn't be —he might as well say good-bye to the chance of that warrant here and now. But he did wonder about that third key. To the shop door perhaps? He walked into the living room, insufferably musty now, that Crocker had called a real tip, and flung open the window.

From the drawers which had been re-filled with their muddled and apparently useless assortment of string and pins and mothballs and coins he collected all the keys that lay amongst it. Fifteen, he counted. Three Yale keys, one Norlond, one stamped R.S.T., one F.G.W. Ltd., seven rusted or otherwise corroded implements for opening the locks of back doors or privy doors or garden gates, a car ignition key and a smaller one, the kind that is used for locking the boot of a car. On both of these last were stamped Citroën double chevron. They had not been together in the same drawer and to neither of them was attached the usual leather tag.

A violent pounding on the front door made him jump. He went out and opened it and saw Lilian Crown standing there.

"Oh, it's you," she said. "Thought it might be kids

got in. Or squatters. Never know these days, do you?"

She wore red trousers and a T-shirt which would have been better suited to Robin. Brash fearlessness is not a quality generally associated with old women, especially those of her social stratum. Timidity, awe of authority, a need for self-effacement so often get the upper hand after the climacteric—as Sylvia might have pointed out to him with woeful examples—but they had not triumphed over Mrs. Crown. She had the boldness of youth, and this surely not induced by gin at ten in the morning.

"Come in, Mrs. Crown," he said, and he shut the door firmly behind her. She trotted about, sniffing.

"What a pong! Haven't been in here for ten years." She wrote something in the dust on top of the chest of drawers and let out a girlish giggle.

His hands full of keys, he said, "Does the name Farriner mean anything to you?"

"Can't say it does." She tossed her dried grass hair and lit a cigarette. She had come to check that the house hadn't been invaded by vandals, come from only next-door, but she had brought her cigarettes with her and a box of matches. To have a companionable smoke with squatters? She was amazing.

"I suppose your niece had a car," he said, and he held up the two small keys.

"Never brought it here if she did. And would've. Never missed a chance of showing off." Her habit of omitting pronouns from her otherwise not particularly economical speech irritated him. He said rather sharply, "Then whom do these keys belong to?"

"No good asking me. If she'd got a car left up in London, what'd she leave her keys about down here for? Oh, no, that car'd have been parked outside for all the world to see. Couldn't get herself a man, so she was always showing what she could get. Wonder who'll get her money? Won't be me, though, not so likely."

She blew a blast of smoke into his face, and he retreated, coughing.

"I'd like to know more about that phone call Miss Comfrey made to you on the Friday evening."

"Like what?" said Mrs. Crown, smoke issuing dragon-like from her nostrils.

"Exactly what you said to each other. You answered the phone and she said, "Hallo, Lilian. I wonder if you know who this is.' Is that right?" Mrs. Crown nodded. "Then what?" Wexford said. "What time was it?"

"About seven. I said hallo and she said what you've said. In a real put-on voice, all deep and la-di-da. 'Of course I know,' I said. 'If you want to know about your dad,' I said, 'you'd best get on to the hospital.' 'Oh, I know all about that,' she said. 'I'm going away on holiday,' she said, 'but I'll come down for a couple of days first.' "

"You're sure she said that about a holiday?" Wexford interrupted.

"Course I'm sure. There's nothing wrong with my memory. Tell you another thing. She called me darling. I was amazed. 'I'll come down for a couple of days first, darling,' she said. Mind you, there was someone else with her while she was phoning. I know what she was up to. She'd got some woman there with her and she wanted her to think she was talking to a man."

"But she called you Lilian."

"That's not to say the woman was in there with her when she started talking, is it? No, if you want to know what I think, she'd got some friend in the place with her, and this friend came in after she'd started talking, so she put in that 'darling' to make her think she'd got a boy friend she was going to see. I'm positive, I knew Rhoda. She said it again, or sort of. 'My dear,' she said. 'Thought you might be worried if you saw lights on, my dear. I'll come in and see you after I've been to the infirmary.' And then whoever it was must have gone out again, I heard a door slam. Her voice went very low after that and she just said in her usual way, 'See you Monday then. Good-bye.' "

"You didn't wish her Many Happy Returns of the day?"

If a spider had shoulders they would have looked like Lilian Crown's. She shrugged them up and down, up and down, like a marionette. "Old Mother Parker told me afterwards it was her birthday. You can't expect me to remember a thing like that. I knew it was in August sometime. Sweet fifty and never been kissed!"

"That's all, Mrs. Crown," said Wexford distastefully and escorted her back to the front door. Sometimes he thought how nice it would be to be a judge so that one could boldly and publicly rebuke people. With his sleeve he rubbed out of the dust the arrowed heart—B loves L—she had drawn there, wondering as he did so if B were the "gentleman friend" she went drinking with, and wondering too about the incidence of adolescent souls lingering on in mangy old carcases.

He made the phone call from home.

"I can tell you that here and now," said Baker. "Dinehart happened to mention it. Rose Farriner runs a Citroën. Any help to you?"

"I think so, Michael. Any news of my Chief Constable's get-together with your Super?"

"You'll have to be patient a bit longer, Reg."

Wexford promised he would be. The air was clearing. Rhoda Rose Comfrey Farriner had made that call to her aunt from Princevale Road on the evening of her birthday when, not unnaturally, she had had a friend with her. A woman, as Lilian Crown had supposed? No, he thought, a man. Late in life, she had at last found herself a man whom she had been attempting to inspire with jealousy. He couldn't imagine why. But never mind. That man, whoever he was, had indeed been inspired, had heard enough to tell him where Rhoda Rose Comfrey Farriner was going on Monday. Wexford had no doubt that that listener had been her killer.

It had been a crime of passion. Adolescent souls linger on, as Mrs. Crown had shown him, in ageing bodies. Not in everyone does the hey-day in the blood grow tame. Had he not himself even recently, good husband though he tried to be, longed wistfully for the sensation of being again in love? Hankered for the feeling of it and murmured to himself the words of Stendhal—though it might be with the ugliest kitchen-maid in Paris, as long as he loved her and she returned his ardour . . .

The girl who sat in the foyer of Kingsmarkham Police Station was attracting considerable attention. Sergeant Camb had given her a cup of tea, and two young detective constables had asked her if she was quite comfortable and was she sure there was nothing they could do to help her? Loring had wondered if it would cost him his job were he to take her up to the canteen for a sandwich or the cheese on toast Chief Inspector Wexford called Fuzz Fondue. The girl looked nervous and upset. She had with her a newspaper at which she kept staring in an appalled way, but she would tell no one what she wanted, only that she must see Wexford.

Her colouring was exotic. There is an orchid, not pink or green or gold, but of a waxen and delicate beige, shaded with sepia, and this girl's face had the hue of such an orchid. Her features looked as if drawn in charcoal on oriental silk, and her hair was black silk, massy and very finely spun. For her countrywomen the sari had been designed, and she walked as if she were accustomed to wearing a sari, though for this visit she was in Western dress, a blue skirt and a white cotton shirt.

"Why is he such a long time?" she said to Loring, and Loring who was a romantic young man thought that it was in just such a tone that the Shunammite had said to the watchmen: Have ye seen him whom my soul loveth?

"He's a busy man," he said, "but I'm sure he won't be long." And for the first time he wished he were ugly old Wexford who could entertain such a visitor in seclusion.

And then, at half-past twelve, Wexford walked in. "Good morning, Miss Patel."

"You remember me!"

Loring had the answer to that one ready. Who could forget her, once seen? Wexford said only that he did remember her, that he had a good memory for faces, and then poor Loring was sharply dismissed with the comment that if he had nothing to do the chief inspector could soon remedy that. He watched beauty and the beast disappear into the lift.

"What can I do for you, Miss Patel?"

She sat down in the chair he offered her. "You're going to be very angry with me. I've done something awful. No, really, I'm afraid to tell you. I've been so frightened ever since I saw the paper. I got on the first train. You're all so nice to me, everyone was so nice, and I know it's going to change and it won't be nice at all when I tell you."

Wexford eyed her reflectively. He remembered that he had put her down as a humourist and a tease, but now her wit had deserted her. She seemed genuinely upset. He decided to try a little humour himself and perhaps put her more at ease.

"I haven't eaten any young women for months now," he said, "and, believe me, I make it a rule never to eat them on Fridays."

She didn't smile. She gave a gulp and burst into tears.

11

He could hardly comfort her as he would have comforted his Sylvia or his Sheila whom he would have taken in his arms. So he picked up the phone and asked for someone to bring up coffee and sandwiches for two, and remarked as much to himself as to her that he wouldn't be able to get angry when he had his mouth full.

Crying did nothing to spoil her face. She wiped her eyes, sniffed and said, "You *are* nice. And I've been such an idiot. I must be absolutely out of my tree."

"I doubt it. D'you feel like beginning, or d'you want your coffee first?"

"I'll get it over."

Should he tell her he was no longer interested in Grenville West, for it must have been he she had come about, or let it go? Might as well hear what it was.

"I told you a deliberate lie," she said.

He raised his eyebrows. "You aren't the first to do that by a long chalk. I could be in the *Guinness Book of Records* as the man who's had more deliberate lies told him than anyone else on earth."

"But I told this one. I'm so ashamed."

The coffee arrived and a plate of ham sandwiches. She took one and held it but didn't begin to eat. "It was about Polly," she said. "Polly never goes out in the evenings alone, but *never*. If she goes to Grenville's, he always runs her home or puts her in a taxi. She had a horrible thing happen about a year back. She was walking along in the dark and a man came up behind her and put his arms round her. She screamed and

88

kicked him and he ran off, but after that she was afraid to be out alone in the dark. She says if people were allowed to have guns in this country she'd have one."

Wexford said gently, "Your deliberate lie, Miss Patel? I think you're stalling."

"I know I am. Oh, dear. Well, I told you Polly was at home with me that Monday evening, but she wasn't. She went out before I got home from work and she came back alone—oh, I don't know, after I was in bed. Anyway, the next day I asked her where she'd been because I knew Grenville was away, and she said she'd got fed up with Grenville and she'd been out with someone else. Well, I knew she'd been unhappy about him for a long time, Grenville, I mean. She wanted to go and live with him. Actually, she wanted to marry him, but he wouldn't even kiss her." Malina Patel gave a little shudder. "Ooh, I wouldn't have wanted him to kiss me! There's something really funny about him, something queer—I don't mean gay-queer, or I don't *think* so—but something sort of hard to . . ."

"On with your story, please, Miss Patel!"

"I'm sorry. So what I was going to say was that Polly had met this man who was married, and that Monday they'd been to some motel and had a room there for the evening. And she said this man of hers was afraid of his wife finding out, she'd put a private detective on him, and if that detective came round, would I say she'd been at home with me?"

"You thought I was a private detective?"

"Yes! I told you I was mad. I told Polly I'd do what she said if a detective came, and a detective did come. It didn't seem so very awful, you see, because it's not a crime, sleeping with someone else's husband, is it? It's not very nice but it's not a crime. I mean, not against the law."

Wexford did his best to suppress his laughter and succeeded fairly well. Those remarks of hers, then, which he had thought witty and made at his expense, had, in fact, come from genuine innocence. If she wasn't so pretty and so sweet, he would have been inclined to call her—it seemed sacrilege—downright stupid.

She ate a sandwich and took a gulp of coffee.

"And I was glad Polly had got someone after being so miserable about Grenville. And I thought private detectives are awful people, snooping and prying and getting paid for doing dirty things like that. So I thought it didn't really matter telling a lie to that sort of person."

This time Wexford had to let his laughter go. She looked at him dubiously over the top of her coffee cup.

"Have you ever known any private detectives, Miss Patel?"

"No, but I've seen lots of them in films."

"Which enabled you to identify me with such ease? Seriously, though. . . ." He stopped smiling. "Miss Flinders knew who I was. Didn't she tell you afterwards?"

It was the crucial question, and on her answer depended whether he accompanied her at once back to Kenbourne Vale or allowed her to go alone.

"Of course she did! But I was too stupid to see. She said you hadn't come about the man and the motel at all, but it was something to do with Grenville and that wallet he'd lost, and she was going to tell me a whole lot more, but I wouldn't *listen*. I was going out, you see, I was late already, and I was sick of hearing her go on and on about Grenville. And she tried again to tell me the next day, only I said not to go on about Grenville, please, I'd rather hear about her new man, and she hasn't mentioned him—Grenville, I mean—since."

He seized on one point. "You knew before that the wallet had been lost, then?"

"Oh yes! She'd been full of it. Long before she told

me about the motel and the man and the private detective. Poor Grenville had lost his wallet on a bus and he'd asked her to tell the police but she hadn't because she thought they wouldn't be able to do anything. That was *days* before she went to the motel."

He believed her. His case for identifying Rhoda Comfrey as Rose Farriner was strengthened. What further questions he asked Malina Patel would be for his amusement only.

"May I ask what made you come and tell me the awful truth?"

"Your picture in the paper. I saw it this morning and I recognised you."

From *that* picture? Frivolous enquiries may lead to humiliation as well as amusement.

"Polly had already gone out. I wished I'd listened to her before. I suddenly realised it had all been to do with that murdered woman, and I realised who you were and everything. I felt awful. I didn't go to work. I phoned and said I'd got gastro-enteritis—which was another lie, I'm afraid—and I left a note for Polly saying I was going to see my mother who was ill, and then I got the train and came here. I've told so many lies now I've almost forgotten who I've told what."

Wexford said, "When you've had more practice you'll learn how to avoid that. Make sure to tell everyone the same lie."

"You don't mean it!"

"No, Miss Patel, I don't. And don't tell lies to the police, will you? We usually find out. I expect we should have found this one out, only we're no longer very interested in that line of enquiry. Another cup of coffee?"

She shook her head. "You've been awfully nice to me."

"You don't go to prison till next time," said Wexford. "What they call a suspended sentence. Come on,

I'll take you downstairs and we'll see if we can fix you up with a lift to the station. I have an idea Constable Loring has to go that way."

Large innocent eyes of a doe or calf met him. "I'm afraid I'm being an awful lot of trouble."

"Not a bit of it," Wexford said breezily. "He'll bear it with the utmost fortitude, believe me."

Once again he got home early with a free evening ahead. Such a thing rarely happened to him in the middle of a murder case. There was nothing to do but wait and wonder. Though not to select or discard from a list of suspects, for he had none, nor attempt to read hidden meanings and calculated falsehoods between the lines of witnesses' statements. He had no witnesses. All he had were four keys and a missing car; a wallet that beyond all doubt now had been lost on a bus; and a tale of a phone call overheard by a man who, against all reasonable probability, loved withered middle-aged gawky Rhoda Comfrey so intensely that he had killed her from jealousy.

Not a very promising collection of objects and negativities and conjectures.

The river was golden in the evening light, having on its shallow rippling surface a patina like that on beaten bronze. There were dragonflies in pale blue or speckled armour, and the willow trailed its hoar leaves in the glassy stream.

"Wouldn't it be nice," said Robin, "if the river went through your garden?"

"My garden would have to be half a mile longer," said Wexford.

Water rats having failed to appear, the little boys had taken off sandals and socks and were paddling. It was fortunate that Wexford, rather against his will, had consented to remove his own shoes, roll up his trousers and join them. For Ben, playing boats with a log of willow wood, leant over too far and toppled in up to his neck. His grandfather had him out before he had time to utter a wail.

"Good thing it's so warm. You'll dry off on the way back."

"Grandad carry."

Robin looked anything but displeased. "There'll be an awful row."

"Not when you tell them how brave Grandad jumped in and saved your brother's life."

"Come *on*. It's only about six inches deep. He'll get in a row and so will you. You know what women are."

But there was no row, or rather, no fresh row to succeed that already taking place. How it had begun Wexford didn't know, but as he and the boys came up to the french windows he heard his wife say with, for her, uncommon tartness, "Personally, I think you've got far more than you deserved, Sylvia. A good husband, a lovely home and two fine healthy sons. D'you think you've ever done anything to merit more than that?"

Sylvia jumped up. Wexford thought she was going to shout some retort at her mother, but at that moment, seeing her mud-stained child, she seized him in her arms and rushed away upstairs with him. Robin, staring in silence, at last followed her, his thumb in his mouth, a habit Wexford thought he had got out of years before.

"And you tell me not to be harsh with her!"

"It's not very pleasant," said Dora, not looking at him, "to have your own daughter tell you a woman without a career is a useless encumbrance when she gets past fifty. When her looks have gone. Her husband only stays with her out of duty and because someone's got to support her."

He was aghast. She had turned away because her eyes had filled with tears. He wondered when he had last seen her cry. Not since her own father died, not for fifteen years.

The second woman to cry over him that day. Coffee and sandwiches were hardly the answer here, though a hug might have been. Instead he said laconically, "I often think if I were a bachelor now at my age, and you were single—which, of course, you wouldn't be— I'd ask you to marry me."

She managed a smile. "Oh, Mr. Wexford, this is so sudden. Will you give me time to think it over?"

"No," he said. "Sorry. We're going out to celebrate our engagement." He touched her shoulder. "Come on. Now. We'll go and have a nice dinner somewhere and then we'll go to the pictures. You needn't tell Sylvia. We'll just sneak out."

"We can't!"

"We're going to."

So they dined at the Olive and Dove, she in an old cotton dress and he in his water-rat-watching clothes. And then they saw a film in which no one got murdered or even got married, still less had children or grandchildren, but in which all the characters lived in Paris and drank heavily and made love all day long. It was half-past eleven when they got back, and Wexford had the curious feeling, as Sylvia came out into the hall to meet them, that they were young lovers again and she the parent. As if she would say, Where had they been and what sort of a time was this to come home? Of course she didn't.

"The Chief Constable's been on the phone for you, Dad."

"What time was that?" said Wexford.

"About eight and then again at ten."

"I can't phone him now. It'll have to wait till the morning."

Sharing the initials and, to some extent, the appearance of the late General de Gaulle, Charles Griswold lived in a converted farmhouse in the village of Millerton—Millerton *les-deux-églises,* Wexford called it privately. Wexford was far from being his favourite officer. He regarded him as an eccentric, and one who used methods of the kind Burden had denounced on Parish Oak station platform.

"I hoped to get hold of you last night," he said coldly when Wexford presented himself at Hightrees Farm at nine-thirty on Saturday morning.

"I took my wife out, sir."

Griswold did not exactly think that policemen shouldn't have wives. He had one himself, she was about the place now, though some said he had more or less mislaid her decades ago. But that females of any kind should so intrude as to have to be taken out displeased him exceedingly. He made no comment. His big forehead rucked up into a frown.

"I sent for you to tell you that this warrant has been sworn. The matter is in the hands of the Kenbourne Police. Superintendent Rittifer foresees entering the house tomorrow morning, and it is entirely by his courtesy that you and another officer may accompany him."

It's my case, Wexford thought resentfully. She was killed in my manor. Oh, Howard, why the hell do you have to be in Tenerife now? Aloud he said, not very politely,

"Why not today?"

"Because it's my belief the damned woman'll turn up today, the way she's supposed to."

"She won't, sir. She's Rhoda Comfrey."

"Rittifer thinks so too. I may as well tell you that if it rested on your notions alone, the obtaining of this warrant wouldn't have my support. I know you. Half the time you're basing your enquiries on a lot of damnfool intuitions and *feelings*."

"Not this time, sir. One woman has positively identified Rhoda Comfrey as Rose Farriner from the photograph. She is the right age, she disappeared at the right time. She complained of appendicitis symptoms only a few months after we know Rhoda Comfrey went to a doctor with such symptoms. She . . ."

"All right, Reg." The Chief Constable delivered the
kind of dismissive shot of which only he was capable.
"I won't say you know your own business best because
I don't think you do."

12

The courtesy of Superintendent Rittifer did not extend
to his putting in an appearance at Princevale Road. No
blame to him for that, Wexford thought. He wouldn't
have done so either in the Superintendent's positi℩
and on a fine Sunday afternoon. For it was two by the
time they got there, he and Burden with Baker and
Sergeant Clements.

Because it was a Sunday they had come up in Burden's car and the traffic hadn't been too bad. Now that
the time had come he was beginning to have qualms,
the seeds of which had been well sown by Burden and
the Chief Constable. The very thing which had first
put him on to Rose Farriner now troubled him. Why
should she go to a doctor and give only to him the
name of Rhoda Comfrey while everyone else knew
her as Rose Farriner? And a local doctor too, one who
lived no more than a quarter of a mile away, who
might easily and innocently mention that other name to
those not supposed to know it. Then there were the
clothes in which Rhoda Comfrey's body had been
dressed. He remembered thinking that his own wife
wouldn't have worn them even in the days when they
were poor. They had been of the same sort of colours
as those sold in the Montfort Circus boutique, but had
they been of anything like the same standard? Would
Mrs. Cohen have wanted to get them at cost and have
described them as "exquisite"? How shaky too had

been that single identification, made by a very young woman who looked anaemic and neurotic, who might even be suffering from some kind of post-natal hysteria.

Could Burden have been right about the wallet? He got out of the car and looked up at the house. Even from their linings he could see that the curtains were of the kind that cost a hundred pounds for a set. The windows were double-glazed, the orange and white paintwork fresh. A bay tree stood in a tub by the front door. He had seen a bay tree like that in a garden centre priced at twenty-five pounds. Would a woman who could afford all that steal a wallet? Perhaps, if she were leading a double life, she had two disparate personalities inside that strong gaunt body. Besides, the wallet had been stolen, and from a bus that passed through Kenbourne Vale . . .

Before Baker could insert the key Mrs. Farriner had given Dinehart, Wexford tested out the two which had been on Rhoda Comfrey's ring. Neither fitted.

"That's a bit of a turn-up for the books," said Burden.

"Not necessarily. I should have brought all the keys that were in that drawer." Wexford could see Baker didn't like it, but he unlocked the door just the same and they went in.

Insufferably hot and stuffy inside. The temperature in the hall must have been over eighty and the air smelt strongly. Not of mothballs and dust and sweat, though, but of pine-scented cleansers and polish and those deodorisers which, instead of deodorising, merely provide a smell of their own. Wexford opened the door to the garage. It was empty. Clean towels hung in the yellow-and-white shower room and there was an unused cake of yellow soap on the washbasin. The only other room on this floor was carpeted in black, and black-and-white geometrically patterned curtains hung at its french window. Otherwise, it contained nothing but two black armchairs, a glass coffee table and a television set.

They went upstairs, by-passing for the time being the first floor and mounting to the top. Here were three bedrooms and a bathroom. One of these bedrooms was totally empty, a second, adjoining it, furnished with a single bed, a wardrobe and a dressing table. Everything was extremely clean and sterile-looking, the wastepaper baskets emptied, the flower vases empty and dry. Again, in this bathroom, there were fresh towels hanging. A medicine chest contained aspirins, nasal spray, sticking plaster, a small bottle of antiseptic. Wexford was beginning to wonder if Rhoda Comfrey had ever stamped anything with her personality, but the sight of the principal bedroom changed his mind.

It was large and luxurious. Looking about him, he recalled that spare room in Carlyle Villas. Since then she had come a long way. The bed was oval, its cover made of some sort of beige-coloured furry material, with furry beige pillows piled at its head. A chocolate-coloured carpet, deep-piled, one wall all mirror, one all glass overlooking the street, one filled with built-in cupboards and dressing table counter, the fourth entirely hung with brown glass beads, strings of them from ceiling to floor. On the glass counter stood bottles of French perfume, a pomander and a crystal tray containing silver brushes.

They looked at the clothes in the cupboards. Dresses and coats and evening gowns hung there in profusion, and all were not only as different from those on Rhoda Comfrey's body as a diamond is different from a ring in a box of Cracker Jacks, but of considerably higher quality than those in Mrs. Farriner's shop.

On the middle floor the living room was L-shaped, the kitchen occupying the space between the arms of the L. A refrigerator was still running on a low mark to preserve two pounds of butter, some plastic-wrapped vegetables and a dozen eggs.

Cream-coloured carpet in the main room, coffee-coloured walls, abstract paintings, a dark red leather suite—real leather, not fake. Ornaments, excluded elsewhere, abounded here. There was a good deal of Chinese porcelain, a bowl that Wexford thought might be Sung, a painting of squat peasants and yellow birds and red and purple splashes that surely couldn't be a Chagall original—or could it?

"No wonder she wanted us to keep an eye on it," said Baker, and Clements began on a little homily, needless in this company, on the imprudence of householders, the flimsiness of locks and the general fecklessness of people who had more money than they knew what to do with.

Wexford cut him short. "That's what I'm interested in." He pointed to a long teak writing desk in which were four drawers and on top of which stood a white telephone. He pictured Rhoda Comfrey phoning her aunt from there, her companion coming in from the kitchen perhaps with ice for drinks. Dr. Lomond had warned her to keep off alcohol. There was plenty of it here in the sideboard, quite an exotic variety, Bacardi and Pernod and Campari as well as the usual whisky and gin. He opened the top drawer in the desk.

A cardboard folder marked *Car* held an insurance policy covering the Citroën, a registration document and a manufacturer's handbook. No driving licence. In another, marked *House,* a second policy and a mass of services bill counterfoils. There was a third folder, marked *Finance,* but it held only a paying-in book from Barclay's Bank, Montfort Circus, W. 19.

"And yet she didn't have a cheque book or a credit card on her," Wexford remarked more or less to himself.

Writing paper in the second drawer, with the address of the house in a rather ornate script. Under the box was a personal phone directory. Wexford turned to C for Comfrey, F for father, D for dad, H for hospital, S for Stowerton, and back to C for Crown. Nothing . . .

Burden said in a curiously high voice, "There's some more stuff here." He had pulled out the drawer in a low table that stood under the window. Wexford moved over to him. A car door banged outside in the street.

"You ought to look at this," Burden said, and he held out a document. But before Wexford could take it there was a sound from below as of the front door being pushed open.

"Not expecting any more of your people, are you?" Wexford said to Baker.

Baker didn't answer him. He and the sergeant went to the head of the stairs. They moved like burglars surprised in the course of robbery, and "burglars" was the first word spoken by the woman who came running up the stairs and stopped dead in front of them.

"Burglars! Don't tell me there's been a break-in!"

She looked round her at the open drawers, the disarranged ornaments. "Mrs. Cohen said the police were in the house. I couldn't believe it, not on the very day I come home." A man had followed her. "Oh, Bernard, look, my God! For heaven's sake, what's happened?"

In a hollow voice, Baker said, "It's quite all right, madam, nothing has been taken, there's been no break-in. I'm afraid we owe you an apology."

She was a tall well-built woman who looked about forty but might have been older. She was handsome, dark, heavily made-up, and she was dressed in expensively tailored denim jeans and waistcoat with a red-silk shirt. The man with her seemed younger, a blond burly man with a rugged face.

"What are you doing with my birth certificate?" she said to Burden.

He handed it to her meekly along with a certificate of a divorce decree. Her face registered many things, mainly disbelief and nervous bewilderment. Wexford said,

"You are Mrs. Rose Farriner?"

"Well, of course I am. Who did you think I was?"

He told her. He told her who he was and why they were there.

"Lot of bloody nonsense," said the man called Bernard. "If you want to make an issue of this, Rosie, you can count on my support. I never heard of such a thing."

Mrs. Farriner sat down. She looked at the photograph of Rhoda Comfrey, she looked at the newspaper Wexford gave her.

"I think I'd like a drink, Bernard. Whisky, please. I thought you were here because burglars had got in, and now you say you thought *I* was this woman. What did you say your name was? Wexford? Well, Mr. Wexford, I am forty-one years old, not fifty, my father has been dead for nine years and I've never been to Kingsmarkham in my life. Thanks, Bernard. That's better. It was a shock, you know. My God, I don't understand how you could make a mistake like that." She passed the documents to Wexford who read them in silence.

Rosemary Julia Golbourne, born forty-one years before in Northampton. The other piece of paper, which was a certificate making a decree nisi absolute, showed that the marriage which had taken place between Rosemary Julia Golbourne and Godfrey Farriner at Christ Church, Lancaster Gate, in April 1959 had been dissolved fourteen years later at Kenbourne County Court.

"Had you delayed another week," said Mrs. Farriner, "I should have been able to show you my second marriage certificate." The blond man rested his hand on her shoulder and glowered at Wexford.

"I can only apologise very profoundly, Mrs. Farriner, and assure you we have done no damage and that everything will be restored as it was."

"Yes, but look here, that's all very well," said Bernard. "You come into my future wife's home, break in more or less, go through her private papers, and all because . . ."

But Mrs. Farriner had begun to laugh. "Oh, it's so ridiculous! A secret life, a mystery woman. And that photograph! Would you like to see what I looked like when I was thirty? For God's sake, there's a picture in that drawer." There was. A pretty girl with dark brown curls, a smiling wide-eyed face only a little softer and smoother than the same face now. "Oh, I shouldn't laugh. That poor creature. But to mix me up with some old spinster who got herself mugged down a country lane!"

"I must say you take it very well, Rosie."

Mrs. Farriner looked at Wexford. She stopped laughing. He thought she was a nice woman, if insensitive. "I shan't take it further, if that's what you're worrying about," she said. "I shan't complain to the Home Secretary. I mean, now I've got over the shock, it'll be something to dine out on, won't it? And now I'll go and make us all some coffee."

Wexford wasn't over the shock. He refused Baker's offer of a lift to Victoria. Burden and he walked slowly along the pavement. Well-mannered as were the residents of Princevale Road, a good many of Mrs. Farriner's neighbours had come out to watch their departure. What some of them were afterwards to call a "police raid" had made their week-end, though they pretended as they watched that they were clipping their hedges or admonishing their children.

The sun shone strongly on Kenbourne Tudor, on subtly-coloured paintwork and unsubtly-coloured flowers, petunias striped and quartered like flags, green plush lawns where sprinklers fountained. Wexford felt hollow inside. He felt that hollow sickness that follows exclusively the making of some hideous howler or *faux pas*.

"There'll be an awful row," said Burden unhelpfully, using the very words Robin had used two days before.

"I suppose so. I should have listened to you."

"Well . . . I didn't say much. It was just that I had this feeling all the time, and you know how I distrust 'feelings.' "

Wexford was silent. They had come to the end of the

street where it joined Montfort Hill. There he said, "What was the feeling? I suppose you can tell me now."

"You've asked me at exactly the right point. O.K., I'll tell you. It struck me the first time we passed this spot." Burden led the chief inspector a little way down Montfort Hill, away from the bus stop they had been making for. "We'll suppose Rhoda Comfrey is on her way to Dr. Lomond's, whose name she's got out of the phone book. She isn't exactly sure where Midsomer Road is, so she doesn't get the bus, she walks from Parish Oak station.

"For some reason which we don't know she doesn't want to give Dr. Lomond her true address, so she has to give him a false one, and one that's within the area of his practice. So far she hasn't thought one up. But she passes these shops and looks up at that tobacconist, and what's the first thing she sees?"

Wexford looked up. "A board advertising Wall's ice cream. My God, Mike, a hanging sign for Player's Number Six Cigarettes. Was that what your feeling was about? Was that why you kept looking back that first time we came in the car? She sees the 'Number Six,' and then that black-and-white street sign for Prince-vale Road?"

Burden nodded unhappily.

"I believe you're right, Mike. It's the way people do behave. It could happen almost unconsciously. Dr. Lomond's receptionist asks her for her address when she comes to register and she comes out with number six, Princevale Road." Wexford struck his forehead with the heel of his hand. "I ought to have seen it! I've come across something like it before, and here in Kenbourne Vale, years ago. A girl called herself Loveday because she'd seen the name on a shop." He turned on Burden. "Mike, you should have told me about this, you should have told me last week."

"Would you have believed me if I had?"

Hot-tempered though he might be, Wexford was a fair man. "I might've—but I'd have wanted to get into that house just the same."

Burden shrugged. "We're back to square one, aren't we?"

13

There was no point in delaying. He went straight to Hightrees Farm. Griswold listened to him with an expression of lipcurling disgust. In the middle of Wexford's account he helped himself to brandy and soda, but he offered nothing to his subordinate.

When it was ended he said, "Do you ever read the newspapers?"

"Yes, sir. Of course."

"Have you ever noticed how gradually over the past ten years or so the press have been ramming it home to people that their basic freedoms are constantly under threat? And who comes in for most of the shit-throwing? The police. You've just given them a big helping of it on a plate, haven't you? All ready for throwing tomorrow morning."

"I don't believe Mrs. Farriner will tell the press, sir."

"She'll tell her friends, won't she? Some busybody dogooder will get hold of it." The Chief Constable (who referred to Mid-Sussex as the general had been in the habit of referring to *La Belle France*—with jealousy and with reverence) said, "Understand, I will not have the hitherto unspotted record of the Mid-Sussex Constabulatory smeared all over by the gutter press. I will not have it endangered by one foolish man who acts on psychology and not on circumstantial evidence."

Wexford smarted under that one. "Foolish man" was

hard to take. And he smarted more when Griswold went on, even though he now called him Reg which meant there would be no immediate retribution.

"This woman's been dead for two weeks, Reg, and as far as you've got, she might as well have dropped from Mars. She might as well have popped off in a space ship every time she left Kingsmarkham." I'm beginning to think she did, Wexford thought, though he said nothing aloud. "You know I don't care to call the Yard in unless I must. By the end of this coming week I'll have to if my own men can't do better than this. It seems to me"—and he gave Wexford a ponderous bull-like glare "—that all you can do is get your picture in the papers like some poove of a film actor."

Sylvia sat in the dining room, the table covered with application forms for jobs and courses.

"You've picked the wrong time of year," her father said, picking up a form that applied for entry to the University of London. "Their term starts next month."

"The idea is I get a job to fill in the year and start doing my degree next year. I have to get a grant, you see."

"My dear, you don't stand a chance. They'll assess you on Neil's salary. At least, I suppose so. He's your husband."

"Maybe he won't be by then. Oh, I'm so sick of you men ruling the world! It's not fair just taking it for granted my husband pays for me like he'd pay for a child."

"Just as fair as taking it for granted the taxpayers will. I know you're not interested in my views or your mother's, but I'm going to give you mine just the same. The way the world still is, women have to prove they're as capable as men. Well, you prove it. Do an external degree or a degree by correspondence and in something that's likely to lead to a good job. It'll take you five years and by that time the boys'll be off your hands. Then when you're thirty-five you and Neil will be two professional people with full-time jobs and a servant you both pay for. Nobody'll treat you like a chattel or a furnisher polisher then. You'll see."

She pondered, looking sullen. Very slowly she began filling in the section of a form headed "qualifications." The list of them, Wexford noted sadly, was sparse. She scrawled a line through *Mr./Mrs./Miss* and wrote *Ms*. Her head came up and the abundant hair flew out.

"I'm glad I've got boys. I'd feel sick with despair for them if they were girls. Didn't you want a son?"

"I suppose I did before Sheila was born. But after she was born, I didn't give it another thought."

"Didn't you think what we'd suffer? You're aware and sensitive, Dad. Didn't you think how we'd be exploited and humiliated by men and *used?*"

It was too much. There she sat, tall and powerful, blooming with health, the youthful hue sitting on her skin like morning dew, a large diamond cluster sparkling on her hand, her hair scented with St. Laurent's *Rive Gauche*. Her sister, described by critics as one of England's most promising young actresses, had a big flat of her own in St. John's Wood where, it had often seemed to her father, she sweetly exploited and used all the men who frequented it.

"I couldn't send you back, could I?" he snapped. "I couldn't give God back your entrance ticket and ask for a male variety instead. I know exactly what Freud felt when he said there was one question that would always puzzle him. What is it that women want?"

"To be people," she said.

He snorted and walked out. The Crockers and a couple of neighbours were coming in for drinks. The doctor hustled Wexford upstairs and produced his sphygmomanometer.

"You look rotten, Reg. What's the matter with you?"

"That's for you to say. How's my blood pressure?"

"Not bad. Is it Sylvia?"

He hated explaining why his daughter and the children were in the house. People categorise others into the limited compartments their imaginations permit. They assumed that either Sylvia or her husband had been unfaithful or that Neil had been cruel. He couldn't spell it all out, but just had to watch the speculating gleam in their eyes and take their pity.

"Partly," he said, "and it's this Comfrey case. I dream about her, Len. I rack my brains, such as they are, about her. And I've made a crazy mistake. Griswold half-crucified me this afternoon, called me a foolish man."

"We all have to fail, Reg," said Crocker like a liberal headmaster.

"There was a sort of sardonic gleam in her eyes when we found her. I don't know if you noticed. I feel as if she's laughing at me from beyond the grave. Hysterical, eh? That's what Mike says I am."

But Mike didn't say it again. He knew when to tread warily with the chief inspector, though Wexford had become a little less glum when there was nothing in the papers on Monday or Tuesday about the Farriner fiasco.

"And that business wasn't all vanity and vexation of spirit," he said. "We've learnt one thing from it. The disappearance of Rhoda Comfrey, alias whatever, may not have been remarked by her neighbours because they expect her to be away on holiday. So we have to wait and hope a while longer that someone from outside will still come to us."

"Why should they at this stage?"

"Exactly because it is at this stage. How long do the majority of people go on holiday for?"

"A fortnight," said Burden promptly.

Wexford nodded. "So those friends and neighbours who knew her under an assumed name would have expected her back last Saturday. Now, they wouldn't have been much concerned if she wasn't back by Sunday, but by Monday when she doesn't answer her phone, when she doesn't turn up for whatever work she does? By today?"

"You've got a point there."

"God knows, every newspaper reader in the country must be aware we still don't know her London identity. The press has rammed it home hard enough. Wouldn't it be nice, Mike, if at this very moment some public-spirited citizen were to be walking into a nick somewhere in north or west London to say she's worried because her boss or the woman next door hasn't come back from Majorca?"

Burden always took Wexford's figurative little flights of fancy literally. "She couldn't have been going there, wouldn't have had a passport."

"As Rhoda Comfrey she might have. Besides, there are all sorts of little tricks you can manage with passports. You're not going to tell me a woman who's fooled us like this for two weeks couldn't have got herself a dozen false passports if she'd wanted them."

"Anyway, she didn't go to Majorca. She came here and got herself stabbed." Burden went to the window and said wonderingly, "There's a cloud up there."

"No bigger than a man's hand, I dare say."

"Bigger than that," said Burden, not recognising this quotation from the Book of Kings. "In fact, there are quite a lot of them." And he made a remark seldom uttered by Englishmen in a tone of hope, still less of astonishment. "It's going to rain."

The room went very dark and they had to switch on the light. Then a golden tree of forked lightning sprang out of the forest, splitting the purple sky. A great rolling clap of thunder sent them retreating from where they had been watching the beginnings of this storm, and Burden closed the windows.

At last the rain came, but sluggishly at first in the way rain always does come when it has held off for weeks, slow intermittent plops of it. Wexford remembered how Sylvia, when she was a tiny child, had believed until corrected that the rain was contained up there in a bag which someone punctured and then finally sliced open. He sat down at his desk and again phoned the Missing Persons Bureau, but no one had been reported missing who could remotely be identified as Rhoda Comfrey.

It was still only the middle of the afternoon. Plenty of time for the public-spirited citizen's anxiety and tension to mount until . . . Today was the day, surely, when that would happen if it was going to happen. The bag was sliced open and rain crashed in a cataract against the glass, bringing with it a sudden drop in the temperature. Wexford actually shivered, for the first time in weeks he felt cold, and he put on his jacket. He found himself seeing the storm as an omen, this break in the weather signifying another break. Nonsense, of course, the superstition of a foolish man. He had thought he had had breaks before, hadn't he? Two of them, and both had come to nothing.

By six no phone calls relevant to Rhoda Comfrey had come in, but still he waited, although it was not necessary for him to be there. He waited until seven, until half-past, by which time all the exciting pyrotechnics of the storm were over and the rain fell dully and steadily. At a quarter to eight, losing faith in his omen, in the importance of this day above other days —it had been one of the dreariest he had spent for a long time—he drove home through the grey rain.

14

It was like a winter's evening. Except at night, the french windows had not been closed since the end of July and now it was 23 August. Tonight they were not only closed, but the long velvet curtains were drawn across them.

"I thought of lighting a coal fire," said Dora who had switched on one bar of the electric heater.

"You've got quite enough to do without that." Child-minding, Wexford thought, cooking meals for five instead of two. "Where's Sylvia gone?" he snapped.

"To see Neil, I think. She said something earlier about presenting him with a final ultimatum."

Wexford made an impatient gesture. He began to walk about the room, then sat down again because pacing can only provoke irritation in one's companion. Dora said,

"What is it, darling? I hate to see you like this."

He shrugged. "I ought to rise above it. There's a story told about St. Ignatius of Loyola. Someone asked him what he would do if the Pope decided to dissolve the Society of Jesus on the morrow, and he said, 'Ten minutes at my orisons and it would be all the same to me.' I wish I could be like that."

She smiled. "I won't ask you if you want to talk about it."

"Wouldn't do any good. I've talked about it to the point of exhaustion—the Comfrey case, that is. As for Sylvia, is there anything we haven't said? I suppose there'll be a divorce, and she'll live here with the boys. I told her this was her home and of course I meant it. I read somewhere the other day that one in three marriages now comes to grief, and hers is going to be one of them. That's all. It just doesn't make me feel very happy."

The phone rang, and with a sigh Dora got up to answer it.

"I'll get it," Wexford said, almost pouncing on the receiver. The voice of Dora's sister calling from Wales as she mostly did on a mid-week evening. He said, yes, there had been a storm and, yes, it was still raining, and then he handed the phone to Dora, deflated. Two weeks before, just a bit earlier than this, he had received the call that told him of the discovery of Rhoda Comfrey's body. He had been confident then, full of hope, it had seemed simple.

Through layers of irrelevant facts, information about people he would never see again and whom he need not have troubled to question, through a mind-clogging jumble of trivia, a gaunt harsh face looked up at him out of his memory, the eyes still holding that indefinable expression. She had been fifty and ugly and shapeless and ill-dressed, but someone had killed her from passion and in revenge. Some man who loved her had believed her to be coming here to meet another man. It was inconceivable, but it must be so. Stabbing in those circumstances is always a crime of passion, the culmination of a jealousy or a rage or an anguish that suddenly explodes. No one kills in that way because he expects to inherit by his victim's death, or thereby to achieve some other practical advantage . . .

"They had the storm in Pembroke this morning," said Dora, coming back.

"Fantastic," said her husband, and then quickly, "Sorry, I shouldn't snipe at you. Is there anything on the television?"

She consulted the paper. "I think I know your tastes by now. If I suggested any of this lot I might get that vase chucked at me. Why don't you read something?"

"What is there?"

"Library books. Sylvia's and mine. They're all down there by your chair."

He humped the stack of them on to his lap. It was easy to sort out which were Sylvia's. Apart from *Woman and the Sexist Plot,* there was Simone de Beauvoir's *The Second Sex* and Mary Wollstonecraft's *A Vindication of the Rights of Woman.* Dora's were a detective story, a biography of Marie Antoinette and Grenville West's *Apes in Hell.* His reaction was to repudiate this last, for it reminded him too forcibly of his first mistake. Women's Lib as seen through the eyes of Shelley's mother-in-law would almost have been preferable. But that sort of behaviour was what Burden called hysterical.

"What's this like?"

"Not bad," said Dora. "I'm sure it's very well-researched. As far as I'm concerned, the title's way-out, quite meaningless."

"It probably refers to an idea the Elizabethans had about unmarried women. According to them, they were destined to lead apes in hell."

"How very odd. You'd better read it. It's based on some play called *The Maid's Tragedy*."

But Wexford, having looked at the portrait of its author, pipe in mouth, on the back of the jacket, turned to Marie Antoinette. For the next hour he tried to concentrate on the childhood and youth of the doomed Queen of France, but it was too real for him, too factual. These events had taken place, they were history. What he needed tonight was total escape. A detective story, however bizarre, however removed from the actualities of detection, was the last thing to give it to him. By the time Dora had brought in the tray with the coffee things, he had again picked up *Apes in Hell*.

Grenville West's biography was no longer of interest to him, but he was one of those people who, before reading a novel, like to acquaint themselves with that short summary of the plot publishers generally display on the front flap of the jacket and sometimes in the preliminary pages. After all, if this précis presents too awful an augury, one need read no further. But in this instance the jacket flap had been obscured by the library's own covering of the book, so he turned the first few pages.

Apparently, it was West's third novel, having been preceded by *Her Grace of Amalfi* and *Arden's Wife*. The plot summary informed him that the author's source had been Beaumont and Fletcher's *The Maid's Tragedy*, a Jacobean drama set in classical Rhodes. West, however, had shifted the setting to the England of his favourite half-timbering and knot gardens, and with an author's omnipotent conjuring trick—his publisher's panegyric, this—had transformed kings and princes into a seventeenth-century aristocracy. Not a bad idea, Wexford thought, and one which Beaumont and Fletcher might themselves have latched on to if writing about one's contemporaries and fellow nationals had been more in favour at the time.

Might as well see what it was like. He turned the page, and his fingers rested on the open pages, his breath held. Then he gave a gasp.

"What on earth is it?" said Dora.

He made her no answer. He was looking at two lines of type in italics on an otherwise blank sheet. The dedication.

For Rhoda Comfrey, without whom this book could never have been written.

15

"Our first red herring," Burden said.

"Only it wasn't a red herring. If this isn't proof West knew her, I don't know what would be. He's known her for years, Mike. This book was published ten years ago."

It was a cool clean day. The rain had washed roofs and pavements and had left behind it a thin mist, and the thermometer on Wexford's wall recorded a sane and satisfactory sixty-five degrees. Burden was back to a normal-weight suit. He stood by the window, closed against the mist, examining *Apes in Hell* with a severe and censorious expression.

"What a load of rubbish," was his verdict. He had read the plot summary. "Ten years ago, yes," he said.

"That Hampton guy, his publisher, why didn't he tell you West had dedicated a book to this woman?"

"Maybe he'd forgotten or he'd never known. I don't know anything about publishing, Mike. For all I know Hampton as West's editor might never see his writer's dedications. In any case, I refuse to believe that a perfectly respectable and no doubt disinterested man like Hampton was involved in a plot to conceal from me West's friendship with Rhoda Comfrey. And the same goes for his literary agent and for Vivian and Polly Flinders. They simply didn't know about the dedication."

"It's a funny thing about the wallet, isn't it?" said Burden after a pause. "He must have given it to her. The alternative is inconceivable."

"The alternative being that he lost it and it was found by chance and deliberately kept by a friend of his? That's impossible, but there's a possibility between those two alternatives, that he left it behind in her house or flat or wherever she lived and she, knowing he was to be away for a month, just kept it for him."

"And *used* it? I don't think much of that idea. Besides, those two girls told you he lost it, and that he asked this Polly to report the loss to the police."

"Are they both lying then?" said Wexford. "Why should they lie?"

Burden didn't answer him. "You'll have him fetched back now, of course."

"I shall try. I've already had a word with the French Police. Commissaire Laquin in Marseilles. We worked together on a case once, if you remember. He's a nice chap."

"I'd like to have heard that conversation."

Wexford said rather coldly, "He speaks excellent English. If West's in the South of France, he'll find him. It shouldn't be too difficult even if he's moving from one hotel to another. He must be producing his passport wherever he goes."

Burden rubbed his chin, gave Wexford the sidelong

look that presages a daring or even outrageous suggestion. "Pity we can't get into West's flat."

"Are you insane? D'you want to see me back on the beat or in the sort of employment Malina Patel marked out for me? Christ, Mike, I can just see us rifling through West's papers and have him come walking in in the middle of it."

"O.K., O.K. You're getting this Laquin to send West home? Suppose he won't come? He may think it a bit thin, fetching him back from his holiday merely because he knew someone who got herself murdered."

"Laquin will ask him to accompany him to a police station and then he'll phone me so that I can speak to West. That'll be a start. If West can give me Rhoda Comfrey's London address he may not need to come home. We'll see. We can't take any steps to enforce his return, Mike. As far as we know, he's committed no offence, and it's quite possible he hasn't seen an English newspaper since he left this country. It's more than likely, if he's that much of a francophile."

Given to *non-sequiturs* this morning, Burden said, "Why couldn't this book have been written without her?"

"It only means she helped him in some way. Did some research for him, I dare say, which may mean she worked in a library. One thing, this dedication seems to show West had no intention of concealing their friendship."

"Let's hope not. So you're going to glue yourself to this phone for the next few days, are you?"

"No," Wexford retorted. "You are. I've got other things to do."

The first should have been to question those girls, but that would have to wait until they were both home in the evening. The second perhaps to visit Silk and Whitebeam in Jermyn Street and discover in detail the circumstances of the purchase of that wallet. And yet wouldn't all be made plain when West was found?

Wexford had a feeling—what anathema that would
have been to the Chief Constable—that West was not
going to be easily found.

He sent Loring back to the leather shop and Bryant
to enquiring of every library in London as to whether
any female member of their staff had not returned to
work after a holiday as she should have done. Then he
took himself to Forest Road.

Young Mrs. Parker with a baby on her hip and old
Mrs. Parker with a potato peeler in her hand looked
at *Apes in Hell* not so much as if it were an historical
novel as an hysterical novelty. Babies and beans might
be all in the day's work to them. Books were not.

"A friend of Miss Comfrey's?" said Stella Parker
at last. It seemed beyond her comprehension that anyone she knew or had known could also be acquainted
with the famous. Grenville West was famous in her
eyes simply because he had his name in print and
had written things which got into print. She repeated
what she had said, this time without the interrogative
note, accepting the incredible just as she accepted nu-
clear fission or the fact that potatoes now cost fifteen
pence a pound. "A friend of Miss Comfrey's. Well!"

Her grandmother-in-law was less easily surprised.
"Rhoda was a go-getter. I shouldn't wonder if she'd
known the Prime Minister."

"But do you know for a fact that she was a friend
of Grenville West's?"

"Speak up."

"He wants to know," said Stella, "if you know if she
knew him, Nanna."

"Me? How should I know. The only West I ever
come across was that Lilian."

Wexford bent over her. "Mrs. Crown?"

"That's right. Her first husband's name was West.
She was Mrs. West when she first come here to live
with Agnes. And poor little John, he was called West
too, of course he was. I thought I told you that, young
man, when we was talking about names that time."

"I didn't ask you," said Wexford.

West is a common name. So he thought as he waited in the car for Lilian Crown to come home from the pub. But if Grenville West should turn out to be some connection by marriage of Rhoda Comfrey's, how much more feasible would any acquaintance between them be. If, for instance, they called each other cousin as many people do with no true blood tie to justify it. Their meeting, their casual affection, would then be explained. And might she not have called herself West, preferring this common though euphonious name over the rarer Comfrey?

She arrived home on the arm of an elderly man whom she did not attempt to introduce to Wexford. They were neither of them drunk, that is to say unsteady on their feet or slurred in their speech, but each reeked of liquor, Lilian Crown of spirits and the old man of strong ale. There was even a dampish look about them, due no doubt to the humid weather, but suggesting rather that they had been dipped into vats of their favourite tipple.

Mrs. Crown evidently wanted her friend to accompany her and Wexford into the house, but he refused with awed protestations and frenetic wobblings of his head. Her thin shoulders went up and she made a monkey face at him.

"O.K., be like that." She didn't say good-bye to him but marched into the house, leaving Wexford to follow her. He found her already seated on the food-stained sofa, tearing open a fresh packet of cigarettes.

"What is it this time?"

He knew he was being over-sensitive with this woman, who was herself totally insensitive. But it was difficult for him, even at his age and after his experiences, to imagine a woman whose only child was a cripple and an idiot not to have had her whole life blighted by her misfortune. And although he sensed that she might answer any questions he asked her about her son with indifference, he still hoped to avoid asking her. Perhaps it was for himself and not for her that he felt this way. Perhaps he was, even now, vulnerable to man's, or woman's, inhumanity.

"You were Mrs. West, I believe," he said, "before you married for the second time?"

"That's right. Ron—Mr. West, that is—got himself killed at Dunkirk." She put it in such a way as to imply that her first husband had deliberately placed himself as the target for a German machine gun or aircraft. "What's that got to do with Rhoda?"

"I'll explain that in a moment, if you don't mind. Mr. West had relatives, I suppose?"

"Of course he did. His mum didn't find him under a gooseberry bush. Two brothers and a sister he had."

"Mrs. Crown, I have good reason to be interested in anyone connected with your late niece who bears the name of West. Did these people have children? Do you know where they are now?" Would she, when she hadn't known the address of her own niece? But very likely they had no reason to be secretive.

"Ethel, the sister, she never spoke a word to me after I married Ron. Gave herself a lot of mighty fine airs, for all her dad was only a farm labourer. Married a Mr. Murdoch, poor devil, and I reckon they'd both be over eighty now if they're not dead. The brothers was Len and Sidney, but Sidney got killed in the war like Ron. Len was all right, I got on O.K. with Len." Mrs. Crown said this wonderingly, as if she had surprised herself by admitting that she got on with anyone connected to her by blood or by marriage. "Him and his wife, they still send me Christmas cards."

"Have they any children?"

Mrs. Crown lit another cigarette from the stub of the last, and Wexford got a blast of smoke in his face. "Not to say *children*. They'll be in their late thirties by now. Leslie and Charley, they're called." The favour in which she held the parents did not apparently extend to their sons. "I got an invite to Leslie's wedding, but he treated me like dirt, acted like he didn't know who

I was. Don't know if Charley's married, wouldn't be bothered to ask. He's a teacher. Fancies himself a cut above his people, I can tell you."

"So as far as you know there isn't a *Grenville* West among them?"

Like Mrs. Parker, Lilian Crown had evidently set him down as stupid. They were both the sort of people who assume authority, any sort of authority, to be omniscient, to know all sorts of private and obscure details of their own families and concerns as well as they know them themselves. This authority did not, and therefore this authority must be stupid. Mrs. Crown cast up her eyes.

"Of course there is. They're all called Grenville, aren't they? It's like a family name, though what right a farm labourer thinks he's got giving his boys a fancy handle like that I never will know."

"Mrs. Crown," said Wexford, his head swimming, "what do you mean, they're all called Grenville?"

She reeled it off rapidly, a list of names. "Ronald Grenville West, Leonard Grenville West, Sidney Grenville West, Leslie Grenville West, Charles Grenville West."

"And these people," he said, half-stunned by it, "your niece Rhoda knew them?"

"May have come across Leslie and Charley when they was little kids, I dare say. She'd have been a lot older."

He had written the names down. He looked at what he had written. Addresses now, and Mrs. Crown was able, remarkably, to provide them or some of them. The parents lived at Myfleet, a village not far from Kingsmarkham, the son Leslie over the county boundary in Kent. She didn't know the whereabouts of Charley, but his school was in South London, so his father said, which meant he must live down there somewhere, didn't it?

And now he had to ask it, as tactfully as he could. For if every male of the West family . . .

"And that is all?" he said almost timorously. "There's no one else called Grenville West?"

"Don't think so. Not that I recall." She fixed him with a hard stare. "Except my boy, of course, but that wouldn't count, him not being normal. Been in a home for the backward like since he was so high. He's called John Grenville West, for what it's worth."

16

No word came from Commissaire Laquin that day. But Loring's enquiries were more fruitful, clearing up at last the matter of the wallet.

"Those girls weren't lying," Wexford said to Burden. "He did lose a wallet on a bus, but it was his *old* one he lost. That's what he told the assistant at Silk and Whitebeam when he went on Thursday, August fourth, to replace it with a new one."

"And yet it was the new one we found in the possession of Rhoda Comfrey."

"Mike, I'm inclined to believe that the old one did turn up and he gave her the new one, maybe on the Saturday when it was too late to tell Polly Flinders. She told him she had reached the age of fifty the day before, and he said O.K., have this for a present."

"You think he was a sort of cousin of hers?"

"I do, though I don't quite see yet how it can help us. All these people on the list have been checked out. Two of them, in any case, are dead. One is in an institution at Myringham, the Abbotts Palmer Hospital. One is seventy-two years old. One had emigrated with his wife to Australia. The last of them, Charles Grenville West, is a teacher, has been married for five years and lives in Carshalton. The father, also John Grenville

West, talks of cousins and second cousins who may bear the name, but he's doddery and vague. He can't tell us the whereabouts of any of them. I shall try this Charles."

Almost the first thing Wexford noticed when he was shown into Charles Grenville West's living room was a shelf of books with familiar titles. *Arden's Wife, Apes in Hell, Her Grace of Amalfi, Fair Wind to Alicante, Killed with Kindness.* They had pride of place in the bookcase and were well-cared for. The whole room was well-cared for, and the neat little house itself, and smiling, unsuspicious, co-operative Mr. and Mrs. West.

On the phone he had told Charles West only that he would like to talk to him about the death of a family connection of his, and West had said he had never met Rhoda Comfrey—well, he might have seen her when he was a baby—but Wexford would be welcome to call just the same. And now Wexford, having accepted a glass of beer, having replied to kind enquiries about the long journey he had made, looked again at the books, pointed to them and said:

"Your namesake would appear to be a favourite author of yours."

West took down *Fair Wind to Alicante.* "It was the name that first got me reading them," he said, "and then I liked them for themselves. I kept wondering if we were related." He turned to the back of the jacket and the author's photograph. "I thought I could see a family resemblance, but I expect that was imagination or wishful thinking, because the photo's not very clear, is it? And then there were things in the books, I mean in the ones with an English setting . . ."

"What sort of things?" Wexford spoke rather sharply. His tone wasn't one to give offence, but rather to show Charles West that these questions were relevant to the murder.

"Well, for instance, in *Killed with Kindness* he describes a manor house that's obviously based on Clythorpe Manor near Myringham. The maze is described and the long gallery. I've been in the house, I know it well. My grandmother was in service there before she was married." Charles West smiled. "My people were all very humble farm workers and the women were all in service, but they'd lived in that part of Sussex for generations, and it did make me wonder if Grenville West was one of us, some sort of cousin, because he seemed to know the countryside so well. I asked my father, but he said the family was so huge and with so many ramifications."

"I wonder you didn't write to Grenville West and ask *him*," said Wexford.

"Oh, I did. I wrote to him care of his publishers and I got a very nice letter back. Would you like to see it? I've got it somewhere." He went to the door and called out, "Darling, d'you think you could find that letter from Grenville West? But he's not a relation," he said to Wexford. "You'll see what he says in the letter."

Mrs. West brought it in. The paper was headed with the Elm Green address. "Dear Mr. West," Wexford read. "Thank you for your letter. It gives me great pleasure that you have enjoyed my novels, and I hope you will be equally pleased with *Sir Bounteous,* which is to be published next month and which is based on Middleton's *A Mad World, My Masters.*

"This novel also has an English setting or, more precisely, a Sussex setting. I am very attached to your native county, and I am sorry to have to tell you that it is not mine, nor can I trace any connection between your ancestry and mine. I was born in London. My father's family came originally from Lancashire and my mother's from the West Country. Grenville was my mother's maiden name.

"So, much as I should have liked to discover some cousins—as an only child of two only children, I have scarcely any living relatives—I must disappoint myself and perhaps you too.

"With best wishes,
"Yours sincerely,
"Grenville West."

With the exception, of course, of the signature, it was typewritten. Wexford handed it back with a shrug. Whatever the information, or lack of it, had done for the author and for Charles West, it had certainly disappointed him. But there was something odd about it, something he couldn't quite put his finger on. The style was a little pretentious with a whisper of arrogance, and in the calculated leading from paragraph to paragraph, the almost too elegant elision of the professional writer. That wasn't odd, though, that wasn't odd at all . . . He was growing tired of all these hints, these "feelings," these pluckings at his mind and at the *fingerspitzengefühl* he seemed to have lost. No other case had ever been so full of whispers that led nowhere. He despised himself for not hearing and understanding them, but whatever Griswold might say, he knew they were sound and true.

"A very nice letter," he said dully. Except, he would have liked to add, that most of it is a carefully spun fabric of lies.

There was one more Grenville West to see, the one who dragged out his life in the Abbotts Palmer Hospital. Wexford tried to picture what that man would be like now, and his mind sickened. Besides, he knew he had only contemplated going there to keep himself away from the police station, away from hearing that Laquin had nothing for him, that Griswold had called in the Yard over his head, for it was getting to the end of the week now, it was Thursday.

That was no attitude for a responsible police officer to take. He went in. The weather was hot and muggy again, and he felt he had gone back a week in time, for there, waiting for him again, was Malina Patel.

An exquisite little hand was placed on his sleeve,

limpid eyes looked earnestly up at him. She seemed tinier and more fragile than ever. "I've brought Polly with me."

Wexford remembered their previous encounters. The first time he had seen her as a provocative tease, the second as an enchanting fool. But now an uneasiness began to overcome his susceptibility. She gave the impression of trying hard to be good, of acting always on impulse, of a dotty and delightful innocence. But was innocent dottiness compatible with such careful dressing, calculated to stun? Could that sweet guilelessness be natural? He cursed those susceptibilities of his, for they made his voice soft and gallant when he said,

"Have you now? Then where is she?"

"In the loo. She said she felt sick and one of the policemen showed her where the loo was."

"All right. Someone will show you both up to my office when she's feeling better."

Burden was there before him. "It would seem, according to your pal, that the whole of France is now being scoured for our missing author. He hasn't been in Annecy, whatever your little nursery rhyme friend may say."

"She's on her way up now, perhaps to elucidate."

The two girls came in. Pauline Flinders' face was greenish from nausea, her lower lip trembling under the ugly prominent teeth. She wore faded frayed jeans and a shirt which looked as if they had been picked out of a crumpled heap on a bedroom floor. Malina too wore jeans, of toffee-brown silk, stitched in white, and a white clinging sweater and gold medallions on a long gold chain.

"I made her come," said Malina. "She was in an awful state. I thought she'd be really ill." And she sat down, having given Burden a shy sidelong smile.

"What is it, Miss Flinders?" Wexford said gently.

"Tell him, Polly. You promised you would. It's silly to come all this way for nothing."

Polly Flinders lifted her head. She said rapidly, in a

monotone, "I haven't had a card from Grenville. That was last year's. The postmark was smudged and I thought you wouldn't know, and you didn't know."

The explosion of wrath she perhaps expected didn't come. Wexford merely nodded. "You also thought I wouldn't know he knew Rhoda Comfrey. But he had known her for years, hadn't he?"

Breathlessly, Polly said, "She helped him with his books. She was there in his flat a lot. But I don't know where she lived. I never asked. I didn't want to know. About the postcard, I . . ."

"Never mind the postcard. Were you and Miss Comfrey in Mr. West's flat on the evening of August fifth?" A nod answered him and a choking sound like a sob. "And you both overheard her make a phone call from there, saying where she would be on the Monday?"

"Yes, but . . ."

"Tell him the truth, Polly. Tell him everything and it'll be all right."

"Very well, Miss Patel, I'll do the prompting." He hadn't taken his eyes from the other girl, and now he said to her, "Have you any idea of Mr. West's present whereabouts? No? I think you told me the lie about the postcard because you were afraid for Mr. West, believing him to have had something to do with Miss Comfrey's death."

She gave him an eager pathetic nod, her hands clenched.

"I don't think we'll talk any more now," he said. "I'll come and see you tomorrow evening. That will give you plenty of time to get into a calmer frame of mind." Malina looked disappointed, less so when he went on, "I shall want you to give me the name of the man with whom you spent that Monday evening. Will you think about that?"

Again she said yes, a sorrowful and despairing monosyllable, and then Burden took them both away, returning to say, "Rhoda Comfrey was blackmailing West. I wonder why we didn't think of that before."

"Because it isn't a very bright idea. I can see how someone might succeed in blackmailing *her*. She had a secret life she genuinely wanted kept secret. But West?"

"West," said Burden repressively, "is almost certainly homosexual. Why else reject Polly? Why else mooch about Soho at night? Why hobnob with all those blokes in bars? And why, most of all, have a long-standing friendship with an older woman on a completely platonic basis? That's the sort of thing these queers do. They like to know women, but it's got to be *safe* women—married ones or women much older than they are."

Wexford wondered why he hadn't thought of that. Once again he had come up against Burden's solid common sense. And hadn't his own "feelings" also been hinting at it when he had read the letter to Charles West?

He jeered mildly just the same. "So this long-standing friend suddenly takes it into her head to blackmail him, does she? After ten years? Threatens to expose his gay goings-on, I suppose." He had never liked the word "queer." "Why should he care? It's nothing these days. He probably advertises his—his inversion in *Gay News*."

"Does he? Then why doesn't your Indian lady friend know about it? Why doesn't his agent or Vivian or Polly? It mightn't do him any good with his readership if ordinary decent people were to find what he gets up to in London at night. It wouldn't with me, I can tell you."

"Since when have you been one of his readers?"

Burden looked a little shamefaced as he always did when confessing to any even mild intellectual lapse. "Since yesterday morning," he admitted. "Got to do something while I'm being a phone operator, haven't I? I sent Loring out to get me two of them in paperback. I thought they'd be above my head, but they weren't. Quite enjoyable, lively sort of stuff, really, and the last thing you'd feel is that their author's homosexual."

"But you say he is."

"And he wants to keep it dark. He's queer but he's still thinking of settling down with Polly—they do that when they get middle-aged—and Rhoda mightn't have liked the idea of only being able to see him with a wife around. So she threatens to spill the beans unless he gives up Polly. And there's your motive."

"It doesn't account for how he happens to have the same name as a whole tribe of her aunt's relatives."

"Look," said Burden, "your Charles West wrote to him, thinking he might be a cousin. Why shouldn't Rhoda have done the same thing years ago, say after she'd read his first book? Charles West didn't pursue it, but she may have done. That could be the reason for their becoming friends in the first place, and then the friendship was strengthened by Rhoda doing research for him for that book that's dedicated to her. The name is relevant only in that it brought them together."

"I just hope," said Wexford, "that tomorrow will bring West and us together."

Robin came up and opened the car door for him.

"Thanks very much," said Wexford. "You're the new hall porter, are you? I suppose you want a tip." He handed over the ices he had bought on the way home. "One for your brother, mind."

"I'll never be able to do it again," said Robin.

"Why's that? School starting? You'll still get in before I do."

"We're going home, Grandad. Daddy's coming for us at seven."

To the child Wexford couldn't express what he felt. There was only one thing he could say, and in spite of his longing to be alone once more with Dora in peace and quiet and orderliness, it was true. "I shall miss you."

"Yes," said Robin complacently. Happy children set a high valuation on themselves. They expect to be loved and missed. "And we never saw the water rat."

"There'll be other times. You're not going to the North Pole."

The little boy laughed inordinately at that one. Wexford sent him off to find Ben and hand the ice over, and then he let himself into the house. Sylvia was upstairs packing. He put his arm round her shoulder, turned her face towards his.

"Well, my dear, so you and Neil have settled your differences?"

"I don't know about that. Not exactly. Only he's said he'll give me all the support I need in taking a degree if I start next year. And he's—he's bought a dishwasher!" She gave a little half-ashamed laugh. "But that's not why I'm going back."

"I think I know why."

She pulled away from him, turning her head. For all her height and her majestic carriage, there was something shy and gauche about her. "I can't live without him, Dad," she said. "I've missed him so dreadfully."

"That's the only good reason for going back, isn't it?"

"The other thing—well, you can say women are equal to men, but you can't give them men's position in the world. Because that's in men's minds, and it'll take hundreds of years to change it." She came out with a word that was unfamiliar to her well-read father. "One would just have to practise aeonism," she said.

What had she been reading now? Before he could ask her, the boys came in.

"We could have a last try for the water rat, Grandad."

"Oh, Robin! Grandad's tired and Daddy's coming for us in an hour."

"An hour," said Robin with a six-year-old's view of time, "is ever so long."

So they went off together, the three of them, over the hill and across the meadow to the Kingsbrook. It was damp and misty and still, the willows bluish amorphous shadows, every blade of grass glistening with water drops. The river had risen and was flowing fast, the only thing in nature that moved.

"Grandad carry," said Ben somewhat earlier in the expedition than usual.

But as Wexford bent down to lift him up, something apart from the river moved. A little way to the right of them, in the opposite bank, a pair of bright eyes showed themselves at the mouth of a hole.

"Ssh," Wexford whispered. "Keep absolutely still."

The water rat emerged slowly. It was not at all rat-like but handsome and almost rotund with spiky fur the colour of seal skin and a round alert face. It approached the water with slow stealth but entered it swiftly and began to swim, spreading and stretching its body, towards the bank on the side where they stood. And when it reached the bank it paused and looked straight at them seemingly without fear, before scurrying off into the thick green rushes.

Robin waited until it had disappeared. Then he danced up and down with delight. "We saw the water rat! We saw the water rat!"

"Ben wants to see Daddy! Ben wants to go home! Poor Ben's feet are cold!"

"Aren't you pleased we saw the water rat, Grandad?"

"Very pleased," said Wexford, wishing that his own quest might come to so simple and satisfying an end.

17

Grenville West's elusiveness could no longer be put down to chance. He was on the run and no doubt had been for nearly three weeks now. Everything pointed to his being the killer of Rhoda Comfrey, and by Friday morning Wexford saw that the case had grown too big for him, beyond the reach of his net. Far from hoping to dissuade the Chief Constable from carrying out his threat, he saw the inevitability of calling in Scotland Yard and also the resources of Interpol. But his call to the Chief Constable left him feeling a little flat, and the harsh voice of Michael Baker, phoning from Kenbourne Vale, made him realise only that now he must begin confessing failure.

Baker asked him how he was, referred to their "red faces" over the Farriner business, then said,

"I don't suppose you're still interested in that chap Grenville West, are you?"

To Wexford it had seemed as if the whole world must be hunting for him, and yet here was Baker speaking as if the man were still a red herring, incongruously trailed across some enormously more significant scent.

"Am I still interested! Why?"

"Ah," said Baker. "Better come up to the Smoke then. It'd take too long to go into details on the phone, but the gist is that West's car's been found in an hotel garage not far from here, and West left the hotel last Monday fortnight without paying his bill."

Wexford didn't need to ask any more now. He remembered to express effusive gratitude, and within not much more than an hour he was sitting opposite Baker at Kenbourne Vale Police Station, Stevens having recovered from his flu or perhaps only his antipathy to London traffic.

"I'll give you a broad outline," said Baker, "and then we'll go over to the Trieste Hotel and see the manager. We got a call from him this morning and I sent Clements up there. West checked in on the evening of Sunday, August seventh and parked his car, a red Citroën, in one of the hotel's lock-up garages. When he didn't appear to pay his bill on Wednesday morning, a chambermaid told Hetherington—that's the manager—that his bed hadn't been slept in for two nights."

"Didn't he do anything about it?" Wexford put in.

"Not then. He says he knew who West was, had his address and had no reason to distrust him. Besides, he'd left a suitcase with clothes in it in his room and his car in the garage. But when it got to the end of the week he phoned West's home, and getting no reply sent someone round to Elm Green. You can go on from there, Sergeant, you talked to the man."

Clements, who had come in while Baker was speaking, greeted Wexford with a funny little half-bow. "Well, sir, this Hetherington, who's a real smoothie but not, I reckon, up to anything he shouldn't be, found out from the girl in that wine bar place where West was, and he wasn't too pleased. But he calculated West would write to him from France."

"Which didn't happen?"

"No, sir. Hetherington didn't hear a word and he got to feeling pretty sore about it. Then, he says, it struck him the girl had said a motoring holiday, which seemed fishy since West's car was still at the Trieste. Also, West had gone off with his room key and hadn't left an ignition key with the hotel. Hetherington began to feel a bit worried, said he suspected foul play, though he didn't get on to us. Instead he went through West's case and found an address book. He got the phone numbers of West's publishers and his agent and Miss Flinders and he phoned them all. None of them could help him, they all said West was in France, so this morning, at long last, he phoned us."

They were driven up to North Kenbourne, round Montfort Circus and down a long street of lofty houses. Wexford noted that Undine Road was within easy walking distance of Parish Oak tube station, and not far, therefore, from Princevale Road and Dr. Lomond's surgery. Formerly the Trieste Hotel had been a gigantic family house, but its balconies and turrets and jutting gables had been masked with new brickwork or weatherboarding, and its windows enlarged and glazed with plain glass. Mr. Hetherington also seemed to have been smoothed out, his sleek fair hair, pink china skin and creaseless suit. He presented as spruce an appearance compared with the four policemen as his hotel did with its neighbours. His careful grooming reminded Wexford of Burden's fastidiousness, though the inspector never quite had the look of having been sprayed all over with satin-finish lacquer.

He took them into his office, a luxurious place that opened off a white-carpeted, redwood panelled hallway in which very large house plants stood about on Corinthian columns.

Neither Baker nor Clements were the sort of men to go in for specious courtesies or obsequious apology. In his rough way, Baker said, "You'll have to tell the whole story again, sir. We're taking a serious view."

"My pleasure." Hetherington flashed a smile that bore witness to his daily use of dental floss, and held it steadily as if for unseen cameras. "I'm feeling considerable concern about Mr. West myself. I feel convinced something dreadful has happened. Do please sit down." He eyed Wexford's raincoat uncertainly, ushered him away from the white upholstered chair in which he had been about to sit, and into a dun-coloured one. He said, "You'll be more comfortable there, I think," as to a caller of low social status directed to the servants' entrance. "Now where shall I begin?"

"At the beginning," said Wexford with perfect gravity. "Go on to the end and then stop."

This time he got an even more uncertain look. "The beginning," said Hetherington, "would be on the Saturday, Saturday the sixth. Mr. West telephoned and asked if he could have a room for three nights, the Sunday, Monday and Tuesday. Naturally, that would usually be an impossible request in August, but it so happened that a very charming lady from Minneapolis who stays with us regularly every year had cancelled on account of . . ." He caught Wexford's eye, stern censor of snobbish digression. "Yes, well, as I say, it happened to be possible, and I told Mr. West he could have Mrs. Gruber's room. He arrived at seven on the Sunday and signed the register. I have it here."

Wexford and Baker looked at it. It was signed "Grenville West" and the Elm Green address was given. Certain that the manager was incapable of obeying his injunction, Wexford said,

"He had been here before, I think?"

"Oh, yes, once before."

"Mr. Hetherington, weren't you surprised that a man who lived within what is almost walking distance of the hotel should want to stay here?"

"Surprised?" said Hetherington. "Certainly not. Why should I be? What business was it of mine? I shouldn't be *surprised* if a gentleman who lived next door wanted to stay in the hotel."

He took the register away from them. While his back was turned Clements murmured with kindly indulgence, "It happens a lot, sir. Men have tiffs with their wives or forget their keys."

Maybe, Wexford thought, but in those cases they don't book their night's refuge some fifteen hours in advance. Even if the others didn't find it odd, he did. He asked Hetherington if West had brought much luggage.

"A suitcase. He may have had a handbag as well." Although Hetherington was strictly correct in employing this word, the rather quaint usage made Wexford want to repeat, in Lady Bracknell's outraged echo, *"A handbag?"* But he only raised his eyebrows, and Hetherington said, "He asked if he could garage his car —he didn't want to leave it on the hardtop parking— so I let him have number five which happened to be vacant. He put the car away himself." There was a small hesitation. "As a matter of fact, it was a little odd now I come to think of it. I offered to get the car garaged for him and asked for his key, but he insisted on doing it himself."

"When did you last see him?" Baker asked.

"I never saw him again. He ordered breakfast in his

room on the Monday morning. No one seems to have seen him go out. I expected him to vacate his room by noon on Wednesday, but he didn't appear to pay his bill." Hetherington paused, then went on to tell the story broadly as Wexford had heard it from Clements. When he had finished Wexford asked him what had become of West's room key.

"Heaven knows. We do stress that our guests hand in their keys at reception when they go out, we make them too heavy to be comfortably carried in a pocket, but it's of no avail. They will take them out with them. We lose hundreds. I have his suitcase here. No doubt you will wish to examine the contents."

For some moments Wexford had been regarding a suitcase which, standing under Hetherington's desk, he had guessed to be the luggage West had left behind him. It was of brown leather, not new but of good quality and stamped inside the lid with the name and crest of Silk and Whitebeam, Jermyn Street. Baker opened it. Inside were a pair of brown whipcord slacks, a yellow roll-neck shirt, a stone-coloured lightweight pullover, a pair of white underpants, brown socks and leather sandals.

"Those were the clothes he arrived in," said Hetherington, his concern for West temporarily displaced by distaste for anyone who would wear trousers with a shiny seat and a pullover with a frayed cuff.

"How about this address book?" said Baker.

"Here."

The entries of names, addresses and phone numbers were sparse. Field and Braybourne, Literary Agents; Mrs. Brenda Nunn's personal address and phone number; several numbers and extensions for West's publishers; Vivian's Vineyard; Polly Flinders; Kenbourne Town Hall; a number for emergency calls to the North Thames Gas Board; London Electricity; The London Library and Kenbourne Public Library, High Road Branch; some French names and numbers and places—and Crown, Lilian, with the Kingsmarkham telephone number of Rhoda Comfrey's aunt.

Wexford said, "Where's the car now?"

"Still in number five garage. I couldn't move it, could I? I hadn't the means."

I wonder if I have, thought Wexford. They trooped out to the row of garages. The red Citroën looked as if it had been well-maintained and it was immaculately polished. The licence plates showed that it was three years old. The doors were locked and so was the boot.

"We'll get that open," Baker said. "Should have a key to fit, or we'll get one. It won't take long."

Wexford felt through the jangling mass in his pocket. Two keys marked with a double chevron. "Try these," he said.

The keys fitted.

There was nothing inside the car but a neat stack of maps of Western Europe on the dashboard shelf. The contents of the boot were more rewarding. Two more brown leather suitcases, larger than the one West had left in his room, and labelled: *Grenville West, Hotel Casimir, Rue Victor Hugo, Paris*. Both were locked, but the opening of suitcases is child's play.

"To hell with warrants," Wexford said out of range of Hetherington's hearing. "Can we have these taken back to the nick?"

"Surely," said Baker, and to Hetherington in the grating tones of admonition that made him unpopular with the public and colleagues alike, "You've wasted our time and the taxpayers' money by delaying like this. Frankly, you haven't a hope in hell of getting that bill paid."

Loring drove the car back with Baker beside him, while Wexford went with Clements. A lunch-time traffic jam held the police car up, Clements taking this opportunity during a lull in events, to expound on lack of public co-operation, laxity that amounted to ob-

struction, and Hetherington's hair which he averred had
been bleached. At last Wexford managed to get him
off this—anyone whose conversation consists in con-
tinual denunciation is wearying to listen to—and on to
James and Angela. By the time they got to the
police station both cases had been opened and were
displayed in the centre of the floor of Baker's drab
and gloomy sanctum.

The cases were full of clothes, some of which had
evidently been bought new for West's holiday. In a
leather bag was a battery operated electric shaver, a
tube of suntan cream and an aerosol of insect re-
pellant, but no toothbrush, toothpaste, soap, sponge or
flannel, cologne or after-shave.

"If he's homosexual," said Wexford, "these are rather odd omissions. I should have expected a fastidious
interest in his personal appearance. Doesn't he even
clean his teeth?"

"Maybe he's got false ones."

"Which he scrubs at night with the hotel nailbrush
and the hotel soap?"

Baker had brought to light a large brown envelope,
sealed. "Ah, the documents." But there was something
else inside apart from papers. Carefully, Baker slit
the envelope open and pulled out a key to which was
attached a heavy wood and metal tag, the metal part
engraved with the name of the Trieste Hotel and the
number of the room West had occupied for one night.

"How about this?" said Baker. "He isn't in France,
he never left the country."

What he handed to Wexford was a British passport, issued according to its cover, to Mr. J. G. West.

18

Wexford opened the passport at page 1.

The name of the bearer was given as Mr. John Grenville West and his national status as that of a citizen of the United Kingdom and Colonies. Page 2 gave West's profession as a novelist, his place of birth as Myringham, Sussex, his date of birth 9 September, 1940, his country of residence as the United Kingdom, his height as five feet, nine, and the colour of his eyes as grey. In the space allotted to the bearer's usual signature, he had signed it *Grenville West*.

The photograph facing this description was a typical passport photograph and showed an apparent lunatic or psychopath with a lock of dark hair grimly falling to meet a pair of black-framed glasses. At the time it was taken, West had sported a moustache.

Page 4 told Wexford that the passport had been issued five years before in London, and on half a dozen of the subsequent pages were stamps showing entries to and exits from France, Belgium, Holland, Germany, Italy, Turkey and the United States, and there was also a visa for the United States. West, he noted, had left the country at least twelve times in those five years.

"He meant to go this time," said Baker. "Why didn't he go? And where is he?"

Wexford didn't answer him. He said to Loring,

"I want you to go now, as fast as you can make it, to the Registry of Births and look up this chap West. You get the volume for the year 1940, then the section with September in, then all the Wests. Have you got that? There'll be a lot of them, but it's unlikely there'll be more than one John Grenville West born on 9 September. I want his mother's name and his father's."

Loring went. Baker was going through the remaining contents of the envelope. "A cheque book," he said, "a Eurocard and an American Express card, travellers' cheques signed by West, roughly a thousand francs. . . . He meant to come back for this lot all right, Reg."

"Of course he did. There's a camera here under some of these clothes, nice little Pentax." Suddenly Wexford wished Burden were with him. He had reached one of those points in a case when, to clear his mind and dispel some of this frustration, he needed Burden and only Burden. For rough argument with no punches pulled, for a free exchange of insults with no offence taken if such words as "hysterical" or "prudish" were hurled in the heat of the moment. Baker was a very inadequate substitute. Wexford wondered how he would react to some high-flown quotation, let alone to being called a pain in the arse. But needs must when the devil drives. Choosing his words carefully, toning down his personality, he outlined to Baker Burden's theory.

"Hardly germane to this enquiry," said Baker, and Wexford's mind went back years to when he and the inspector had first met and when he had used those very words. "All this motive business. Never mind motive. Never mind whether West was this Comfrey woman's second cousin or, for that matter, her grandmother's brother-in-law." A big-toothed laugh at this witticism. "It's all irrelevant. If I may say so, Reg—" Like all who take offence easily, Baker never minded giving offence to others or even noticed he was giving it. "If I may say so, you prefer the trees to the woods. Ought to have been one of these novelist chappies yourself. Plain facts aren't your cup of tea at all."

Wexford took the insult—for it is highly insulting to be told that one would be better at some profession other than that which one has practised for forty years —without a word. He chuckled to himself at Baker's mixed metaphors, sylvan and refective. Was refective the word? Did it mean what he thought it did, pertaining to mealtimes? There was another word he had meant to look up. It was there, but not quite there, on the tip of his tongue, the edge of his memory. He needed a big dictionary, not that potty little Concise Oxford which, in any case, Sheila had appropriated long ago . . .

"Plain facts, Reg," Baker was saying. "The principal plain fact is that West scarpered on the day your Comfrey got killed. I call that evidence of guilt. He meant to come back to the Trieste and slip off to France, but something happened to scare him off."

"Like what?"

"Like being seen by someone where he shouldn't have been. That's like what. That's obvious. Look at that passport. West wasn't born in London, he was born somewhere down in your neck of the woods. There'll be those around who'll know him, recognise him." Baker spoke as if the whole of Sussex were a small rural spot, his last sentence having a *Wind in the Willows* flavour about it as if West had been the Mole and subject to the scrutiny of many bright eyes peering from the boles of trees. "That's where these second cousins and grandmother's whatsits come in. One of them saw him, so off into hiding he went."

"Under the protection, presumably, of another of them?"

"Could be," said Baker seriously. "But we might just as well stop speculating and go get us a spot of lunch. You can't do any more. I can't do any more. You can't find him. I can't find him. We leave him and his gear to the Yard, and that's that. Now how about a snack at the Hospital Arms?"

"Would you mind if we went to Vivian's Vineyard instead, Michael?"

With some casting up of eyes and pursing of lips, Baker agreed. His expression was that of a man who allows a friend with an addiction one last drink or cigarette. So on the way to Elm Green Wexford was

obliged to argue it out with himself. It seemed apparent
that West had booked into the Trieste to establish an
alibi, but it was a poor sort of alibi since he had
signed the register in his own name. Baker would have
said that all criminals are fools. Wexford knew this
was often not so, and especially not so in the case of
the author of books praised by critics for their
historical accuracy, their breadth of vision and their
fidelity to their models. He had not meant to kill her,
this was no premeditated crime. On the face of it, the
booking in to the Trieste looked like an attempt at
establishing an alibi, but it was not. For some other
purpose West had stayed there. For some other reason
he had gone to Kingsmarkham. How had his car keys
come into Rhoda Comfrey's possession? And who was
he? Who was he? Baker called that irrelevant, yet
Wexford knew now the whole case and its final
solution hung upon it, upon West's true identity and
his lineage.

It was true that he couldn't see the woods for the
trees, but not that he preferred the latter. Here the
trees would only coalesce into a woods when he
could have each one before him individually and
then, at last, fuse them. He walked in a whispering
forest, little voices speaking to him on all sides, hinting
and pleading—"Don't you see now? Can't you put
together what he has said and she has said and what
I am saying?"

Wexford shook himself. He wasn't in a whispering
wood but crossing Elm Green where the trees had all
been cut down, and Baker was regarding him as if he
had read in a medical journal that staring fixedly at
nothing, as Wexford had been doing, may symptomise
a condition akin to epilepsy.

"You O.K., Reg?"

"Fine," said Wexford with a sigh, and they went
into the brown murk of Vivian's Vineyard. The girl
with the pale brown face sat on a high stool behind

the bar, swinging long brown legs, chatting desultorily to three young men in what was probably blue denim, though in here it too looked brown. The whole scene might have been a sepia photograph.

Baker had given their order when Victor Vivian appeared from the back with a wine bottle in each hand.

"Hallo, hallo, hallo!" He came over to their table and sat down in the vacant chair. Today the T-shirt he wore was printed all over with a map of the vineyards of France, the area where his heart was being covered by Burgundy and the Auvergne.

"What's happened to old Gren, then? I didn't know a thing about it, you know, till Rita here gave me the lowdown. I mean, told me there was this hotel chap after him in a real tizz, you know."

Baker wouldn't have replied to this but Wexford did. "Mr. West didn't go to France," he said. "He's still in this country. Have you any idea where he might go?"

Vivian whistled. He whistled like the captain of the team in the *Boys' Own Paper*. "I say! Correct me if I'm wrong, you know, but I'm getting your drift. I mean, it's serious, isn't it? I mean, I wasn't born yesterday."

From a physical point of view this was apparent, though less so from Vivian's mental capacity. Not for the first time Wexford wondered how a man of West's education and intelligence could have borne to spend more than two minutes in this company unless he had been obliged to. What had West seen in him? What had he seen, for that matter, in Polly Flinders, dowdy and desperate, or in the unprepossessing, graceless Rhoda Comfrey?

"You reckon old Gren's on the run?"

The girl put two salads, a basket of rolls and two glasses of wine in front of them. Wexford said, "You told me Mr. West came here fourteen years ago. Where did he come from?"

"Couldn't tell you that, you know. I mean, I didn't come here myself till a matter of five years back. Gren was here. *In situ,* I mean."

"You never talked about the past? About his early life?"

Vivian shook his head, his beard waggling. "I'm not one to push myself in where I'm not wanted, you know. Gren never talked about any family. I mean, he may have said he'd lost his parents—I think he did say that, you know, I think so."

"He never told you where he'd been born?"

Baker was looking impatient. If it is possible to eat ham and tomatoes with an exasperated air, he was doing so. And he maintained a total disapproving silence.

Vivian said vaguely, "People don't, you know. I mean, I reckon Rita here was born in Jamaica, but I don't know, you know. I don't go about telling people where I was born. Gren may have been born in France, you know, France wouldn't surprise me." He banged his chest. "Old Gren brought me this T-shirt back from his last holiday, you know. Always a thoughtful sort of chap. I mean, I don't like to think of him in trouble, I don't at all."

"Did you see him leave for this holiday of his? I mean . . ." How easy it was to pick up the habit! "When he left here on Sunday, the seventh?"

"Sure I did. He popped in the bar. About half six it was, you know. 'I'm just off, Vic,' he says. He wouldn't have a drink, you know, on account on having a long drive ahead of him. I mean, his car was parked out here in the street, you know, and I went out and saw him off. 'Back on September fourth,' he says, and I remember I thought to myself, his birthday's round about then, I thought, eighth or the ninth, you know, and I thought I'd look that up and check and have a bottle of champers for him."

"Can you also remember what he was wearing?"

"Gren's not a snappy dresser, you know. I mean,

he went in for those roll-neck jobs, seemed to like them, never a collar and tie if he could get away with it, I mean. His old yellow one, that's what he was wearing, you know, and a sweater and kind of dark-coloured trousers. Never one for the gear like me, you know. I'd have sworn he went to France, I mean I'd have taken my oath on it. This is beyond me, frankly, you know. I'm lost. When I think he called out to me, 'I'll be in Paris by midnight, Vic,' in that funny high voice of his, and he never went there at all—well, I go cold all over, you know. I mean, I don't know what to think."

Baker could stand no more. Abruptly he said, "We'll have the bill, please."

"Sure, yes, right away. Rita! When he turns up—well, if there's anything I can do, you know, any sort of help I can give, you can take that as read, you know. I mean, this has knocked me sideways."

It was evident that Baker thought the representatives of the Mid-Sussex Constabulary would return to their rural burrow almost at once. He had even looked up the time of a suitable train from Victoria and offered a car to take them there. Wexford hardened himself to hints—there were so many other hints he would have softened to if he had known how—and marched boldly back into the police station where Loring sat patiently waiting for him.

"Well?"

"Well, sir, I've found him." Loring referred to his notes. "The birth was registered at Myringham. In the county," he said earnestly, "of Sussex, 9 September 1940. John Grenville West. His father's name is given as Ronald Grenville West and his mother's as Lilian West, born Crawford."

19

Little John. Sweet affectionate little love, the way them mongols are . . . Mrs. Parker's voice was among the whisperers. He could hear it clearly in the receiver of his mind, and hear too Lilian Crown's, brash and tough and uncaring. Been in a home for the backward like since he was so high . . .

"I looked up the parents too, sir, just to be on the safe side. Ronald West's parents were John Grenville West and Mary Ann West, and Ronald's birth was also registered in Myringham in 1914. The mother, Lilian West, was the daughter of William and Agnes Crawford, and her birth was registered in Canterbury in 1917. Ronald and Lilian West were married in Myringham in 1937."

"You're sure there's no other John Grenville West born on that date and registered at Myringham?"

How could there be? Such a coincidence would evince the supernatural.

"Quite sure, sir," said Loring.

"I know who this man is. He's mentally retarded. He's been in an institution for the greater part of his life." Wexford was uncertain whom he was addressing. Not Baker or Loring or the baffled Clements. Perhaps only himself. "It can't be!" he said.

"It is, sir," said Loring, not following, anxious only that his thoroughness should not be questioned.

Wexford turned from him and buried his face in his hands. Burden would have called this hysterical or maybe just melodramatic. For Wexford, at this moment, it was the only possible way of being alone. Fantastic pictures came to him of a normal child being classified as abnormal so that his mother, in order to make a desired marriage, might be rid of him. Of that child somehow acquiring an education, of being adopted but retaining his true name. They why should Lilian Crown have concealed it?

He jumped up. "Michael, may I use your phone?"

"Sure you can, Reg."

Baker had ceased to hint, had stopped his impatient fidgeting. Wexford knew what he was thinking. It was as if there had been placed before him, though invisible to others, a manual of advice to ambitious policemen. Always humour the whims of your chief's uncle, even though in your considered opinion the old boy is off his rocker. The uses of nepotism must always be borne in mind when looking to promotion.

Burden's voice, from down there in the green country, sounded sane and practical and encouraging.

"Mike, could you get over to the Abbotts Palmer Hospital? Go there, don't phone. I could do that myself. They have, or had, an inmate called John Grenville West. See him if you can."

"Will do," said Burden. "Is he seeable? What I'm trying to say is, is he some sort of complete wreck or is he capable of communicating?"

"If he's who he seems to be, he's more than capable of communicating, in which case he won't be there. But I'm not sending you on a wild goose chase. You have to find out when he entered the institution, when he left and how. Everything you can about him. O.K.? And if you find he's not there but was cured, if that's possible, and went out into the world, confront the man's mother with it, will you? You may have to get tough with her. Get tough. Find out if she knew he was Grenville West, the author, and why the hell she didn't tell us."

"Am I going to find out who his mother is?"

"Mrs. Lilian Crown, 2, Carlyle Villas, Forest Road."

"Right," said Burden.

"I'll be here. I'd come back myself, only I want

to wait in Kenbourne till Polly Flinders gets home this evening."

Baker accepted this last so philosophically as to send down for coffee. Wexford took pity on him.

"Thanks, Michael, but I'm going to take myself off for a walk." He said to Loring, "You can get over to All Souls' Grove and find out when the Flinders girl is expected home. If Miss Patel is taking another of her days off, I dare say you won't find the work too arduous."

He went out into the hazy sunshine. Sluggishly people walked, idled on street corners. It seemed strange to him, as it always does to us when we are in a state of turbulence, that the rest of humanity was unaffected. He that is giddy thinks the world turns round. Giddiness exactly described his present condition, but it was a giddiness of the mind, and he walked steadily and slowly along Kenbourne High Road. At the cemetery gate he turned into the great necropolis. Along the aisles, between the serried tombs, he walked, and sat down at last on a toppled gravestone. On a warm summer's day there is no solitude to be found on a green or in a park, but one may always be sure of being alone in the corner of a cemetery. The dead themselves seem to decree silence, while the atmosphere of the place and its very nature are repellent to most people.

Very carefully and methodically he assembled the facts, letting the whispers wait. West had been cagey about his past, had made few friends, and those he had were somehow unsuitable and of an intellect unequal to his own. He gave his publishers and his readers his birthplace as London, though his passport and the registration of his birth showed he had been born in Sussex. His knowledge of the Sussex countryside and its great houses also showed a familiarity with that county. No one seemed to know anything of his life up to fourteen years before, when he had first come to Elm Green and two years before his first book was published. Not to his neighbour and intimate friend did he ever speak of his origins, and to one other bearer of the name Grenville West he had denied any connection with the family.

Why?

Because he had something to keep hidden, while Rhoda Comfrey was similarly secretive because she had her blackmailing activities to keep hidden. Put the two together and what do you get? A threat on the part of the blackmailer to disclose something. Not perhaps that West was homosexual—Wexford could not really be persuaded that these days this was of much significance —but that he had never been to a university (as his biography claimed he had), never been a teacher or a courier or a free-lance journalist, been indeed nothing till the age of twenty-four when he had somehow emerged from a home for the mentally handicapped.

As his first cousin, Rhoda Comfrey would have known it; from her it could never have been kept as it had been kept from others. Had she used it as a final weapon—Burden's theory here being quite tenable— when she saw herself losing her cousin to Polly Flinders? West had overheard that phone call made by her to his own mother, even though she had called Lilian Crown "Darling" to put him off the scent. Had he assumed that she meant to see his mother and wrest from her the details of his early childhood, the opinions of doctors, all Mrs. Crown's knowledge of the child's incarceration in that place and his subsequent release?

Here, then, was a motive for the murder. West had booked into the Trieste Hotel because it was simpler to allow Polly Flinders and Victor Vivian to believe him already in France. But that he had booked in his own name and for three nights showed surely that he had never intended to kill his cousin. Rather he had meant to use those three days for argument with Rhoda and to attempt to dissuade her from her intention.

But how had he done it? Not the murder, that might be clear enough, that unpremeditated killing in a fit of angry despair. How had he contrived in the first place such an escape and then undergone such a metamorphosis? Allowing for the fact that he might originally have been unjustly placed in the Abbotts Palmer or its predecessor, how had he surmounted his terrible difficulties? Throughout his childhood and early youth he must have been there, and if not in fact retarded, retardation would surely have been assumed for some years so that education would have been withheld and his intellect dulled and impeded by the society of his fellow inmates. Yet at the age of twenty-five or -six he had written and published a novel which revealed a learned knowledge of the Elizabethan drama, of history and of the English usage of the period.

If, that is, he were he.

It couldn't be, as Wexford had said to Loring, and yet it must be. For though John Grenville West might not be the author's real name, though he might for a suitable pseudonym by chance have alighted on it—inventing it, so to speak, himself—other aspects were beyond the possibility of coincidence. True, the chance use of this name (instead, for example, of his real one which might be absurd or dysphonious) could have brought him and Rhoda together, the cousinship at first having been assumed on her part as Charles West had also assumed it. But he could not by chance have also chosen her cousin's birthday and parentage. It must be that John Grenville West, the novelist, the francophile, the traveller, was also John Grenville West, the retarded child his mother had put away when he was six years old. From this dismal state, from this position in the world . . .

He stopped. The words he had used touched a bell and rang it. Again he was up in the spare bedroom with his daughter, and Sylvia was talking about men and women and time, saying something about men's position in the world. And after that she had said this position could only be attained by practising something or other. Deism? No, of course not. Aeolism? Didn't that mean being long-winded? Anyway, it wasn't that, she hadn't said that. What had she said?

He tried placing one letter of the alphabet after another to follow the diphthong and the O, and settled at last with absolute conviction for 'aeonism'. Which must have something to do with aeons. So she had only meant that, in order for sexual equality to be perfected, those who desired it would have to transcend the natural course of time.

He felt disappointed and let down, because, with a curious shiver in that heat, he had felt he had found the key. The word had not been entirely new to him. He fancied he had heard it before, long before Sylvia spoke it, and it had not meant transcending time at all.

Well, he wasn't getting very far cogitating like this. He might as well go back. It was after five, and by now Burden might have got results. He left the cemetery as they were about to close the gates and got a suspicious look from the keeper who had been unaware of his presence inside. But outside the library he thought of that elusive word again. He had a large vocabulary because in his youth he had always made a point of looking up words whose meaning he didn't know. It was a good rule and not one reserved to the young.

This was the place for which Grenville West had a ticket and where Wexford himself had first found his books. Now he spared them a glance on his way to the reference room. Four were in, including *Apes in Hell,* beneath whose covers Rhoda Comfrey's name lurked with such seeming innocence.

The library had only one English dictionary, the *Shorter Oxford* in two bulky volumes. Wexford took the first one of these down, sat at the table and opened it. "Aeolism" was not given, and he found that "aeolistic" meant what he thought it did and that it was an invention of Swift's. "Aeon" was there—*An age, or the whole duration of the world, or of the universe; an immeasurable period of time; eternity.* "Aeonian" too and "aeonial," but no "aeonism."

Could Sylvia have made it up, or was it perhaps the etymologically doubtful brain child of one of her favourite Women's Lib writers? That wouldn't account for his certainty that he had himself previously come across it. He replaced the heavy tome and crossed the street to the police station.

Baker was on the phone when he walked in, chatting with such tenderness and such absorption that Wexford guessed he could only be talking to his wife. But the conversation, though it appeared only to have been about whether he would prefer fried to boiled potatoes for his dinner and whether he would be home by six or could make it by ten to, put him in great good humour. No, no calls had come in for Wexford. Loring had not returned, and he, Baker, thought it would be a good idea for the two of them to adjourn at once to the Grand Duke. Provided, of course, that this didn't delay him from getting home by ten to six.

"I'd better stay here, Michael," Wexford said rather awkwardly, "if that's all right with you."

"Be my guest, Reg. Here's your young chap now."

Loring was shown in by Sergeant Clements. "She came in at half-past four, sir. I told her to expect you some time after six-thirty."

He had no idea what he would say to her, though he might have if only Burden would phone. The word still haunted him. "Would you mind if I made a call?" he said to Baker.

Humouring him had now become Baker's line. "I said to be my guest, Reg. Do what you like." His wife and the fried potatoes enticed him irresistibly. "I'll be off then." With stoical resignation, he added, "I dare say we'll be seeing a good deal of each other in the next few days."

Wexford dialled Sylvia's number. It was Robin who answered.

"Daddy's taken Mummy up to London to see Auntie Sheila in a play."

The Merchant of Venice at the National. She was playing Jessica, and her father had seen her in the part a month before. Another of those whispers hissed at him from the text—"But love is blind, and lovers cannot see the pretty follies that themselves commit." To the boy he said,

"Who's with you, then? Grandma?"

"We've got a sitter," said Robin. "For Ben," he added.

"See you," said Wexford just as laconically, and put the receiver back. Clements was still there, looking, he thought, rather odiously sentimental. "Sergeant," he said, "would you by any chance have a dictionary in this place?"

"Plenty of them, sir. Urdu, Bengali, Hindi, you name it, we've got it. Have to have on account of all these immigrants. Of course we do employ interpreters, and a nice packet they make out of it, but even they don't know all the words. And just as well, if you ask me. We've got French too and German and Italian for our Common Market customers, and common is the word. Oh, yes, we've got more Dick, Tom and Marias, as my old father used to call them, than they've got down the library."

Wexford controlled an impulse to throw the phone at him. "Would you have an *English* dictionary?"

He was almost sure Clements would say this wasn't necessary as they all spoke English, whatever the hoi-polloi might do. But to his surprise he was told that they did and Clements would fetch it for him, his pleasure.

He hadn't been gone half a minute when the switch-board, with many time-wasting enquiries, at last put through a call from Burden. He sounded as if the afternoon had afforded him work that had been more distressing than arduous.

"Sorry I've been so long. I'm not so tough as I think I am. But, God, the sights you see in these places. What it boils down to is that John Grenville West left the Abbotts Palmer when he was twenty . . ."

"What?"

"Don't get excited," Burden said wearily. "Only because they hadn't the facilities for looking after him properly. He isn't a mongol at all, whatever your Mrs. Parker said. He was born with serious brain damage and one leg shorter than the other. Reading between the lines, from what they said and didn't say, I gather this was the result of his mother's attempt to procure an abortion."

Wexford said nothing. The horror was all in Burden's voice already.

"Don't let anyone ever tell me," said the inspector savagely, "that it is wrong to legalise abortion."

Wexford knew better than to say at this moment that it was Burden who had always told him, and others, that. "Where is he now?"

"In a place near Eastbourne. I went there. He's been nothing more than a vegetable for eighteen years. I suppose the Crown woman was too ashamed to tell you. I've just come from her. She said it was ever so sad, wasn't it, and offered me a gin."

20

The dictionaries Clements brought him, staggering under their weight, turned out to be the *Shorter Oxford* in its old vast single volume and *Webster's International* in two volumes.

"There's a mighty lot of words in those, sir. I doubt if anyone's taken a look at them since we had that

nasty black magic business in the cemetery a couple of
years back and I couldn't for the life of me remember
how to spell mediaeval."

It was the associative process which had led Rhoda
Comfrey to give Dr. Lomond her address as 6, Prince-
vale Road, and that same process that had brought
Sylvia's obscure expression back to Wexford's mind.
Now it began to operate again as he was looking
through the *Addenda and Corrigenda* to the *Shorter
Oxford*.

"Mediaeval?" he said. "You mean you weren't
sure whether there was a diphthong or not?" The
sergeant's puzzled frown made him say hastily, "You
weren't sure whether it was spelt i,a,e or i,e, was that
it?"

"Exactly, sir." Clements' need to put the world
right—or to castigate the world—extended even to
criticising lexicographers. "I don't know why we can't
have simplified spelling, get rid of all these unnecessary
letters. They only confuse schoolkids, I know they
did me. I well remember when I was about twelve
. . ."

Wexford wasn't listening to him. Clements went on
talking, being the kind of person who would never
have interrupted anyone when he was speaking, but
didn't think twice about assaulting a man's ears while
he was reading.

". . . And day after day I got kept in after school for
mixing up 'there' and 'their,' if you know what I mean,
and my father said . . ."

Diphthongs, thought Wexford. Of course. That ae
was just an anglicisation of Greek *eeta,* wasn't it, or
from the Latin which had a lot of ae's in it? And often
these days the diphthong was changed to a single e, as
in the modern spelling, medieval. So his word, Sylvia's
word, might appear among the E's and not the A's at
all. He heaved the thick wedge of pages back to the
E section. "Eolienne—A fine dress fabric . . ." "Eosin
—A red dye-stuff . . .

Maybe Sylvia's word had never had a diphthong, maybe it didn't come from Greek or Latin at all, but from a name or a place. That wasn't going to help him, though, if it wasn't in the dictionaries. Wild ideas came to him of getting hold of Sylvia here and now, of calling a taxi and having it take him down over the river to the National Theatre, finding her before the curtain went up in three-quarters of an hour's time . . . But there was still another dictionary.

"Harassment, now," the sergeant was saying. "There's a word I've never been able to spell, though I always say over to myself, 'possesses possesses five s's.'"

Webster's International. He didn't want it to be international, only sufficiently comprehensive. The E section. "Eocene," "Eolienne"—and there it was.

"Found what you're looking for, sir?" said Clements.

Wexford leaned back with a sigh and let the heavy volume fall shut. "I've found, Sergeant, what I've been looking for for three weeks."

Rather warily, Malina Patel admitted them to the flat. Was it for Loring's benefit that she had dressed up in harem trousers and a jacket of some glossy white stuff, heavily embroidered? Her black hair was looped up in complicated coils and fastened with gold pins.

"Polly's in an awful state," she said confidingly. "I can't do anything with her. When I told her you were coming I thought she was going to faint, and then she cried so terribly. I didn't know what to do."

Perhaps, Wexford thought, you could have been a friend to her and comforted her, not spent surely a full hour making yourself look like something out of a seraglio. There was no time now, though, to dwell on forms of hypocrisy, on those who will seek to present themselves as pillars of virtue and archetypes of beauty even at times of grave crisis.

Making use of those fine eyes—could she even cry at will?—she said sweetly, "But I don't suppose you want to talk to me, do you? I think Polly will be up to seeing you. She's in there. I said to her that everything would be all right if she just told the truth, and then you wouldn't frighten her. Please don't frighten her, will you?"

Already the magic was working on Loring who looked quite limp. It had ceased to work on Wexford.

"I'd rather frighten you, Miss Patel," he said. Her eyelashes fluttered at him. "And you're wrong if you think I don't want to talk to you. Let us go in here."

He opened a door at random. On the other side of it was a squalid and filthy kitchen, smelling of strong spices and of decay, as if someone had been currying meat and vegetables that were already rotten. The sink was stacked up to the level of the taps with unwashed dishes. She took up her stand in front of the sink, too small to hide it, a self-righteous but not entirely easy smile on her lips.

"You're very free with your advice," he said. "Do you find in your experience that people take it?"

"I was only trying to help," she said, slipping into her little girl role. "It was good advice, wasn't it?"

"You didn't take my good advice."

"I don't know what you mean."

"Not to lie to the police. The scope of the truth, Miss Patel, is very adequately covered by the words of the oath one takes in the witness box. I swear to tell the truth, the whole truth and nothing but the truth. After I had warned you, you obeyed—as far as I know—the first injunction and the third but not the second. You left out a vital piece of truth."

She seized on only one point. "I'm not going into any witness box!"

"Oh, yes, you will. One thing you may be sure of is that you will. Yesterday morning you received a phone call, didn't you? From the manager of the Trieste Hotel."

She said sullenly, "Polly did."

"And when Miss Flinders realised that Mr. West's car had been found, you told her that the police

would be bound to find out. Did you advise her to
tell us? Did you remember my advice to you? No. You
suggested that the best thing would be to bring her to
us with the old story that your conscience had been
troubling you."

She shifted her position, and the movement sent
the dirty plates subsiding over the edge of the bowl.

"When did you first know the facts, Miss Patel?"

A flood of self-justification came from her. Her
voice lost its soft prettiness and took on a near-
cockney inflexion. She was shrill.

"What, that Polly hadn't been in a motel with a
married man? Not till last night. I didn't, I tell you,
I didn't till last night. She was in an awful state and
she'd been crying all day, and she said I can't tell him
that man's address because there isn't a man. And that
made me laugh because Polly's never had a real boy
friend all the time I've known her, and I said, You
made it up? And she said she had. And I said, I bet
Grenville never kissed you either, did he? So she cried
some more and . . ." The faces of the men told her she
had gone too far. She seemed to remember the personality she wished to present and to grab at it in the
nick of time. "I knew you'd find out because the police
always did, you said. I warned her you'd come, and
then what was she going to say?"

"I meant," Wexford tried, "when did you know
where Miss Flinders had truly been that night?"

Anxiety gone—he wasn't really cross, men would
never really be cross with her—she smiled the amazed
smile of someone on whom a great revelatory light
has shone. "What a weird thing! I never thought about
that."

No, she had never thought about that. About her
own attractions and her winning charm she had thought,
about establishing her own ascendancy and placing her
friend in a foolish light, about what she called her
conscience she had thought but never about the aim of

all these enquiries. What a curiously inept and deceiving term Freud had coined, Wexford reflected, when he named the conscience the superego!

"It never occurred to you then that a girl who never went out alone after dark must have had some very good reason for being out alone all that evening and half the night? You didn't think of that aspect? You had forgotten perhaps that that was the evening of Rhoda Comfrey's murder?"

She shook her head guilelessly. "No, I didn't think about it. It couldn't have had anything to do with me or Polly."

Wexford looked at her steadily. She looked back at him, her fingers beginning to pick at the gold embroideries on the tunic whose whiteness set off her orchid skin. At last the seriousness of his gaze affected her, forcing her to use whatever powers of reasoning she had. The whole pretty sweet silly facade broke, and she let out a shattering scream.

"Christ," said Loring.

She began to scream hysterically, throwing back her head. The heroine, Wexford thought unsympathetically, going mad in white satin. "Oh, slap her face or something," he said and walked out into the hall.

Apart from the screeches, and now the choking sounds and sobs from the kitchen, the flat was quite silent. It struck him that Pauline Flinders must be in the grip of some overpowering emotion, or stunned into a fugue, not to have reacted to those screams and come out to enquire. He looked forward with dread and with distaste to the task ahead of him.

All the other doors were closed. He tapped on the one that led to the living room where he had interviewed her before. She didn't speak, but opened the door and looked at him with great sorrow and hopelessness. Everything she wore and everything about her seemed to drag her down, the flopping hair, the stooping shoulders, the loose overblouse and the long skirt, compelling the eye of the beholder also to droop and fall.

Today there was no script on the table, no paper in the typewriter. No book or magazine lay open. She had been sitting there waiting—for how many hours? —paralysed, capable of no action.

"Sit down, Miss Flinders," he said. It was horrible to have to torture her, but if he was to get what he wanted he had no choice. "Don't try to find excuses for not telling me the name of the man you spent the evening of August eighth with. I know there was no man."

She tensed at that and darted him a look of terror, and he knew why. But he let it pass. Out of pity for her, his mind was working quickly, examining this which was so fresh to him, so recently realised, trying to get enough grasp on it to decide whether the whole truth need come out. But even at this stage, with half the facts still to be understood, he knew he couldn't comfort her with that one.

She hunched in a chair, the pale hair curtaining her face. "You were afraid to go out alone at night," he said, "and for good reason. You were once attacked in the dark by a man, weren't you, and very badly frightened?"

The hair shivered, her bent body nodded.

"You wished it were legal in this country for people to carry guns for protection. It's illegal too to carry knives, but knives are easier to come by. How long is it, Miss Flinders, since you have been carrying a knife in your handbag?"

She murmured, "Nearly a year."

"A flick knife, I suppose. The kind with a concealed blade that appears when you press a projection on the hilt. Where is that knife now?"

"I threw it into the canal at Kenbourne Lock."

Never before had he so much wished he could leave someone in her position alone. He opened the door and called to Loring to come in. The girl bunched her lips over her teeth, straightened her shoulders, her face very white.

"Let us at least try to be comfortable," said Wexford, and he motioned her to sit beside him on the sofa while Loring took the chair she had vacated. "I'm going to tell you a story." He chose his words carefully. "I'm going to tell you how this case appears."

"There was a woman of thirty called Rhoda Comfrey who came from Kingsmarkham in Sussex to London where she lived for some time on the income from a football pools win, a sum which I think must have been in the region of ten thousand pounds.

"When the money began to run out she supplemented it with an income derived from blackmail, and she called herself West, Mrs. West, because the name Comfrey and her single status were distasteful to her. After some time she met a young man, a foreigner, who had no right to be in this country but who, like Joseph Conrad before him, wanted to live here and write his books in English. Rhoda Comfrey offered him an identity and a history, a mother and father, a family and a birth certificate. He was to take the name of someone who would never need national insurance or a passport because he had been and always would be in an institution for the mentally handicapped—her cousin, John Grenville West. This the young man did.

"The secret bound them together in a long uneasy friendship. He dedicated his third novel to her, for it was certain that without her that book would never have been written. He would not have been here to write it. Was he Russian perhaps? Or some other kind of Slav? Whatever he was, seeking asylum, she gave him the identity of a real person who would never need to use his reality and who was himself in an asylum of a different kind.

"And what did she get from him? A young and personable man to be her escort and her companion. He was homosexual, of course, she knew that. All the better. She was not a highly-sexed woman. It was not love and satisfaction she wanted, but a man to show off to observers.

"How disconcerting for her, therefore, when he took on a young girl to type his manuscripts for him, and that young girl fell in love with him. . . ."

Polly Flinders made a sound of pain, a single soft, "Ah!" perhaps irrepressible. Wexford paused, then went on.

"He wasn't in love with her. But he was growing older, he was nearly middle-aged. What sort of dignified future has a homosexual who follows the kind of life-style he had been following into his forties? He decided to marry, to settle down—at least superficially—to add another line to that biography of his on the back of his books.

"Perhaps he hadn't considered what this would mean to the woman who had created him and received his confidences. It was not she, twelve years his senior, he intended marrying, but a girl half her age. To stop him, she threatened to expose his true nationality, his illegalities and his homosexual conduct. He had no choice but to kill her."

Wexford looked at Polly Flinders who was looking hard at him.

"But it wasn't quite like that, was it?" he said.

21

While he was speaking a change had gradually come over her. She was suffering still but she was no longer tortured with fear. She had settled into a kind of resigned repose until, at his last sentence, apprehensiveness came back. But she said nothing, only nodding her head and then shaking it, as if she wished to please him, to agree with him, but was doubtful whether he wanted a yes or a no.

"Of course he had a choice," Wexford went on. "He could have married and left her to go ahead. His readers would have felt nothing but sympathy with a man who wanted asylum in this country, even though he had used illegal means to get it. And there was not the slightest chance of his being deported after so long. As for his homosexuality, who but the most old-fashioned would care? Besides, the fact of his marriage would have put paid to any such aspersion. And where and how would Rhoda Comfrey have published it? In some semi-underground magazine most of his readers would never see? In a gossip column where it would have to be written with many circumlocutions to avoid libel? Even if he didn't feel that *any* publicity is good publicity, he still had a choice. He could have agreed to her demands. Marriage for him was only an expedient, not a matter of passion."

The girl showed no sign that these words had hurt her. She listened calmly, and now her hands lay folded in her lap. It was as if she were hearing what she wanted to hear but had hardly dared hope she would. Her pallor, though, was more than usually marked. Wexford was reminded of how he had once read in some legend or fairy story of a girl so fair and with skin so transparent, that when she drank, the course the red wine followed could be seen as it ran down her throat. But Polly Flinders was in no legend or fairy story—or even nursery rhyme—and her dry bunched lips looked parched for wine or love.

"It was for this reason," he said, "that someone else was alarmed—the girl he could so easily be prevented from marrying. She loved him and wanted to marry him, but she knew that this older woman had far more influence over him than she did.

"August fifth was Rhoda Comfrey's birthday. Grenville West showed her—and showed the girl too—how

little malice or resentment he felt towards her by giving
her an expensive wallet for a birthday present. In-
dicating, surely, that he meant to let her rule him? That
evening they were all together, the three of them, in
Grenville West's flat, and Rhoda Comfrey asked if she
might make a phone call. Now when a guest does that,
a polite host leaves the room so that the person making
the call may be private. You and Mr. West left the
room, didn't you, Miss Flinders? But perhaps the door
was left open.

"She was only telephoning her aunt to say she was
going to visit her father in Stowerton Infirmary on the
following Monday, but to impress you and Mr. West
she made it appear as if she were talking to a man.
You were uninterested in that aspect of it, but you
were intrigued to find out where she would be on the
Monday. In the country where you could locate her as
you never could on her own in London."

He paused, deciding to say nothing about the
Trieste Hotel and West's disappearance, guessing that
she would be thankful for his name to be omitted.

"On the evening of Monday, August eighth, you went
to Stowerton, having found out when visiting time
was. You saw Miss Comfrey get on a bus with another
woman, and you got on too, without letting her
see you. You left the bus at the stop where she left it
and followed her across the footpath—intending what?
Not to kill her then. I think you wished only to be
alone with her to ask why and to try to dissuade her
from interfering between you and Mr. West.

"But she laughed at you, or was patronising, or something of that sort. She said something hurtful and cruel,
and driven beyond endurance, you stabbed her. Am I
right, Miss Flinders?"

Loring sat up stiffly, bracing himself, waiting perhaps
for more screams. Polly Flinders only nodded. She
looked calm and thoughtful as if she had been asked
for verbal confirmation of some action, and not even a

reprehensible action, she had performed years before. Then she sighed.

"Yes, that's right. I killed her. I stabbed her and wiped the knife on the grass and got on another bus and then a train and came home. I threw the knife into Kenbourne Lock on the way back. I did it just like you said." She hesitated, added steadily, "And why you said."

Wexford got up. It was all very civilised and easy and casual. He could tell what Loring was thinking. There had been provocation, no real intent, no premeditation. The girl realised all this and that she would get off with three or four years, so better confess it now and put an end to the anxiety that had nearly broken her. Get it over and have peace, with no involvement for Grenville West.

"Pauline Flinders," he said, "you are charged with the murder on August eighth of Rhoda Agnes Comfrey. You are not obliged to say anything in answer to the charge, but anything you do say may be taken down and used in evidence."

"I don't want to say anything," she said. "Do I have to go with you now?"

"It seems," said Burden when Wexford phoned him, "a bit of a sell."

"You want more melodrama? You want hysterics?"

"Not exactly that. Oh, I don't know. There seems to have been so many oddities in this case, and what it all boils down to is that it was this girl all along. She killed the woman just because she was coming between her and West." Wexford said nothing. "I suppose she *did* kill her? She's not confessing in an attempt to protect West?"

"Oh, she killed her all right. No doubt about that. In her statement she's given us the most precise circumstantial account of times, the geography of the Forest Road area, what Rhoda Comfrey was wearing and even the fact that the London train, the 9:24 Kingsmarkham to Victoria, was ten minutes late that night. Tomorrow Rittifer will have Kenbourne Lock dragged and we'll find that knife."

"And West himself had nothing to do with it?"

"He had everything to do with it. Without him there'd have been no problem. He was the motive. I'm tired now, Mike, and I've got another call to make. I'll tell you the rest after the special court tomorrow."

His other call was to Michael Baker. A woman with a soft voice and a slight north country accent answered. "It's for you, darling," she called out, and Baker called back, "Coming, darling." His voice roughened, crackling down the phone when he heard who it was, and implicit in his tone was the question, "Do you know what time it is?" though he didn't actually say this. But when Wexford had told him the bare facts he became immediately cocky and rather took the line that he had predicted such an outcome all along.

"I knew you were wasting your time with all those names and dates and birth certificates, Reg. I told you so." Wexford had never heard anyone utter those words in seriousness before, and had he felt less tired and sick he would have laughed. "Well, all's well that ends well, eh?"

"I dare say. Good night, Michael."

Maybe it was because he forgot to add something on the lines of his eternal gratitude for all the assistance rendered him by Kenbourne Police that Baker dropped the receiver without another word. Or, rather, without more than a fatuous cry of, "Just coming, sweetheart," which he hardly supposed could be addressed to him.

Dora was in bed, sitting up reading the Marie Antoinette book. He sat down beside her and kicked off his shoes.

"So it's all over, is it?" she said.

"I've behaved very badly," he muttered. "I've strung that wretched girl along and told her lies and accepted lies from her just to get a confession. I've got a horrible job. She still thinks she's got away with it."

"Darling," Dora said gently, "you do realise I haven't the least idea what you're talking about?"

"Yes, in a way I'm talking to myself. Maybe being married is talking to oneself with one's other self listening."

"That's one of the nicest things you've ever said to me."

He went into the bathroom and looked at his ugly face in the glass, at the bags under his tired eyes and the wrinkles and the white stubble on his chin that made him look like an old man.

"I am alone the villain of the earth," he said to the face in the glass, "and feel I am so most."

In court on Saturday morning, Pauline Flinders was charged with the murder of Rhoda Comfrey, committed for trial and remanded in custody.

After it was over Wexford avoided the Chief Constable—it was supposed to be his day off, wasn't it?—and gave Burden the slip and pretended not to see Dr. Crocker, and got into his own car and drove to Myringham. What he had to do, would spend most of the day doing, could only be done in Myringham.

He drove over the Kingsbrook Bridge and through the old town to the centre. There he parked on the top floor of the multi-storey car park, for Myringham was given over to shoppers' cars on Saturdays, and went down in the lift to enter the building on the opposite side of the street.

In marble this time, Edward Edwards, a book in his hand, looked vaguely at him. Wexford paused to read what was engraved on the plinth and then went in, the glass doors opening of their own accord to admit him.

22

For years before it became a hotel—for centuries even
—the Olive and Dove had been a coaching inn where
the traveller might not get a bedroom or, come to
that, a bed to himself, but might be reasonably sure
of securing a private parlour. Many of these parlours,
oak-panelled, low-ceilinged cubbyholes, still remained,
opening out of passages that led away from the bar
and the lounge bar, though they were private no
longer but available to any first comer. In the smallest
of them where there was only one table, two chairs
and a settle, Burden sat at eight o'clock on Sunday
evening, waiting for the chief inspector to come and
keep the appointment he had made himself. He
waited impatiently, making his half-pint of bitter last,
because to leave the room now for another drink would
be to invite invasion. Coats thrown over tables imply
no reservation in the Olive at week-ends. Besides, he
had no coat. It was too warm.

Then at ten past, when the bitter was down to its
last inch, Wexford walked in with a tankard in each
hand.

"You're lucky I found you at all, hidden away like
this," he said. "This is for plotters or lovers."

"I thought you'd like a bit of privacy."

"Maybe you're right. I am Sir Oracle, and when I
ope my lips let no dog bark."

Burden raised his tankard and said, "Cheers! This
dog's going to bark. I want to know where West is, why
he stayed at that hotel, who he is, come to that,
and why I had to spend Friday afternoon inspecting
mental hospitals. That's for a start. I want to know why,

on your own admission, you told that girl two entirely false stories and where you spent yesterday."

"They weren't entirely false," said Wexford mildly. "They had elements of the truth. I knew by then that she had killed Rhoda Comfrey because there was no one else who could have done so. But I also knew that if I presented her with the absolute truth at that point, she would have been unable to answer me, and not only should I not have got a confession, but she would very likely have become incoherent and perhaps have collapsed. What was true was that she was in love with Grenville West, that she wanted to marry him, that she overheard a phone conversation and that she stabbed Rhoda Comfrey to death on the evening of August eighth. All the rest, the motive, the lead-up to the murder and the characters of the protagonists to a great degree—all that was false. But it was a version acceptable to her and one which she might not have dreamed could be fabricated. The sad thing for her is that the truth must inevitably be revealed and has, in fact, already been revealed in the report I wrote yesterday for Griswold.

"I spent yesterday in the new public library in Myringham, in the reference section, reading Havelock Ellis, a biography of Chevalier d'Éon, and bits of the life histories of Isabelle Eberhardt, James Miranda Barry and Martha Jane Burke—if those names mean anything to you."

"There's no need to be patronising," said Burden. "They don't."

Wexford wasn't feeling very light-hearted, but he couldn't, even in these circumstances, resist teasing Burden who was already looking irritable and aggrieved.

"Oh, and Edward Edwards," he said. "Know who Edward Edwards was? The Father of Public Libraries, it said underneath his statue. Apparently, he was instrumental in getting some bill through Parliament in 1850 and . . ."

"For God's sake," Burden exploded, "can't you get

on to West? What's this Edwards got to do with West?"

"Not much. He stands outside libraries and West's books are inside."

"Then where *is* West? Or are you saying he's going to turn up now he's read in the paper that one of his girl friends has murdered the other one?"

"He won't turn up."

"Why won't he?" Burden said slowly. "Look, d'you mean there were two people involved in murdering Rhoda Comfrey? West as well as the girl?"

"No. West is dead. He never went back to the Trieste Hotel because he was dead."

"I need another drink," said Burden. In the doorway he turned round and said scathingly, "I suppose Polly Flinders bumped him off too?"

"Yes," said Wexford. "Of course."

The Olive was getting crowded and Burden was more than five minutes fetching their beer. "My God," he said, "who d'you think's out there? Griswold. He didn't see me. At least, I don't think so."

"Then you'd better make that one last. I'm not running the risk of bumping into him."

Burden sat down again, his eye on the doorway which held no door. He leant across the table, his elbows on it. "She can't have. What became of the body?"

Wexford didn't answer him directly. "Does the word eonism mean anything to you?"

"No more than all those names you flung at me just now. Wait a minute, though. An aeon means a very long time, an age. An aeonist is—let's see—is someone who studies changes over long periods of time."

"No. I thought something like that too. It has nothing to do with aeons, there's no 'a' in it. Havelock Ellis coined the word in a book published in 1928 called *Studies in the Psychology of Sex, Eonism and other Studies*. He took the name from that of the Chevalier d'Éon—Charles Éon de Beaumont—who died in this country in the early part of the nineteenth century—" Wexford paused and said, ". . . having masqueraded for thirty-three years as a woman.

"Rhoda Comfrey masqueraded for twenty years as a man. When I agreed that Pauline Flinders had murdered Grenville West, I meant that she had murdered him in the body of Rhoda Comfrey. Rhoda Comfrey and Grenville West were one and the same."

"That's not possible," said Burden. "People would have known or at least suspected." Intently staring at Wexford's face, he was oblivious of the long bulky shadow that had been cast across the table and his own face.

Wexford turned round, said, "Good evening, sir," and smiled pleasantly. It was Burden who, realising, got to his feet.

"Sit down, Mike, sit down," said the Chief Constable, casting upon Wexford a look that implied he would have liked the opportunity to tell him to sit down also. "May I join you? Or is the chief inspector here indulging his well-known habit of telling a tale with the minimum of celerity and the maximum of suspense? I should hate to interrupt before the climax was reached."

In a stifled voice, Burden said, "The climax was reached just as you came in, sir. Can I get you a drink?"

"Thank you, but I have one." Griswold produced, from where he had been holding it, for some reason, against his trouser leg, a very small glass of dry sherry. "And now I too would like to hear this wonderful exposition, though I have the advantage over you, Mike, of having read a condensed version. I heard your last words. Perhaps you'll repeat them."

"I said she couldn't have got away with it. Anyone she knew well would have known."

"Well, Reg?" Griswold sat down on the settle next to Burden. "I hope my presence won't embarrass you. Will you go on?"

"Certainly I will, sir." Wexford considered saying

he wasn't easily embarrassed but thought better of it.
"I think the answer to that question is that she took
care, as we have seen, only to know *well* not very
sensitive or intelligent people. But even so, Malina
Patel had noticed there was something odd about Grenville West, and she said she wouldn't have liked him
to kiss her. Even Victor Vivian spoke of a 'funny
high voice' while, incidentally, Mrs. Crown said that
Rhoda's voice was deep. I think it probable that such
people as Oliver Hampton and Mrs. Nunn did
know, or rather, if they didn't know she was a woman,
they suspected Grenville West of being of ambivalent
sex, of being physically a hermaphrodite, or maybe an
effeminate homosexual. But would they have told me?
When I questioned them I suspected West of nothing
more than being acquainted with Rhoda Comfrey.
They are discreet people, who were connected with
West in a professional capacity. As for those men
Rhoda consorted with in bars, they wouldn't have been
a bunch of conservative suburbanites. They'd have
accepted her as just another oddity in a world of
freaks.

"Before you came in, sir, I mentioned three
names. Isabelle Eberhardt, James Miranda Barry and
Martha Jane Burke. What they had in common was
that they were all eonists. Isabelle Eberhardt became
a nomad in the North African desert where she was
in the habit of sporadically passing herself off as male.
James Barry went to medical school as a boy in the
days before girls were eligible to do so, and served
for a lifetime as an army doctor in the British Colonies.
After her death she was found to be a woman, and
a woman who had had a child. The last named is
better known as Calamity Jane who lived with men as
a man, chewed tobacco, was proficient in the use of
arms, and was only discovered to be a woman while
she was taking part in a military campaign against
the Sioux.

"The Chevalier d'Éon was a physically normal man

who successfully posed as a female for thirty years.
For half that period he lived with a woman friend
called Marie Cole who never doubted for a moment
that he also was a woman. She nursed him through
his last illness and didn't learn he was a man until
after his death. I will quote to you Marie Cole's reaction
to the discovery from the words of the Notary Public,
Doctors' Commons, 1810. 'She did not recover from
the shock for many hours.'

"So you can see that Rhoda Comfrey had precedent
for what she did, and that the lives of these predecessors
of hers show that cross-dressing succeeds in its aim.
Many people are totally deceived by it, others specu-
late or doubt, but the subject's true sex is often not
detected until he or she becomes ill or is wounded,
or until, as in Rhoda's case, death supervenes."

The Chief Constable shook his head, as one who
wonders rather than denies. "What put you on to it,
Reg?"

"My daughters. One saying a woman would have to
be an eonist to get a man's rights, and the other
dressing as a man on the stage. Oh, and Grenville
West's letter to Charles West—that had the feel of
having been written by a woman. And Rhoda's fingernails painted but clipped short. And Rhoda having a
toothbrush in her luggage at Kingsmarkham and West
not having one in his holiday cases. All feelings, I'm
afraid, sir."

"That's all very well," said Burden, "but what
about the age question? Rhoda Comfrey was fifty and
West was thirty-eight."

"She had a very good reason for fixing her age as
twelve years less than her true one. I'll go into that
in a minute. But also you must remember that she saw
herself as having lost her youth and those best years.
This was a way of regaining them. Now think what
are the signs of youth in men and women. A woman's
subcutaneous fat begins to decline at fifty or there-
abouts, but a man never has very much of it. So even

a young man may have a hard face, lined especially under the eyes without looking older than he is. A woman's youthful looks largely depend on her having no lines. Here, as elsewhere, we apply a different standard for the sexes. You're what, Mike? In your early forties? Put a wig and make-up on you and you'll look an old hag, but cut off the hair of a woman of your age, dress her in a man's suit, and she could pass for thirty. My daughter Sheila's twenty-four, but when she puts on doublet and hose for Jessica in *The Merchant of Venice* she looks sixteen."

Remarkably, it was the Chief Constable who supported him. "Quite true. Think of Crippen's mistress, Ethel Le Neve. She was a mature woman, but when she tried to escape across the Atlantic disguised in men's clothes she was taken for a youth. And by the way, Reg, you might have added Maria Marten, the Red Barn victim, to your list. She left her father's house disguised as a farm labourer, though I believe transvestism was against the law at the time."

"In seventeenth-century France," said Wexford, "men, at any rate, were executed for it."

"Hmm. You have been doing your homework. Get on with the story, will you?"

Wexford proceeded, "Nature had not been kind to Rhoda as a woman. She had a plain face and a large nose and she was large-framed and flat-chested. She was what people call 'mannish,' though incidentally no one did in this case. As a young girl she tried wearing ultra-feminine clothes to make herself more attractive. She copied her aunt because she saw that her aunt got results. She, however, did not, and she must have come to see her femaleness as a grave disadvantage.

"Because she was female she had been denied an education and was expected to be a drudge. All her miseries came from being a woman, and she had none of a woman's advantages over a man. My daughter Sylvia complains that men are attentive to her because of her physical attractions but accord her no respect as a person. Rhoda had no physical attractions so, because she was a woman, she received neither attention nor respect. No doubt she would have stayed at home and become an embittered old maid, but for a piece of luck. She won a large sum of money in an office football pools syndicate. Where she first lived in London, and whether as a man or a woman, I don't know and I don't think it's relevant. She began to write. Did she at this time cease to wear those unsuitable clothes and take to trousers and sweaters and jackets instead? Who knows? Perhaps, dressed like that, she was once or twice mistaken for a man, and that gave her the idea. Or what is more likely, she took to men's clothes because, as Havelock Ellis says, cross-dressing fulfilled a deep demand of her nature.

"It must have been then that she assumed a man's name, and perhaps this was when she submitted her first manuscript to a publisher. It was then or never, wasn't it? If she was going to have a career and come into the public eye there must be no ambivalence of sex.

"By posing—or passing—as a man she had everything to gain: the respect of her fellows, a personal feeling of the rightness of it for her, the freedom to go where she chose and do what she liked, to walk about after dark in safety, to hobnob with men in bars on an equal footing. And she had very little to lose. Only the chance of forming close intimate friendships, for this she would not dare to do—except with unobservant fools like Vivian."

"Well," said Burden, "I've just about recovered from the shock, unlike Marie Cole who took some hours. But there's something else strikes me she had to lose." He looked with some awkwardness in the direction of the Chief Constable, and Griswold, without waiting for him to say it, barked, "Her sexuality, eh? How about that?"

"Len Crocker said at the start of this case that some people are very low-sexed. And if I may again quote Havelock Ellis, eonists often have an almost asexual disposition. 'In people,' he says, 'with this psychic anomaly, physical sexual urge seems often subnormal.' Rhoda Comfrey, who had had no sexual experience, must have decided it was well worth sacrificing the possibility—the remote possibility—of ever forming a satisfactory sexual relationship for what she had to gain. I am sure she did sacrifice it and became a man whom other men and women just thought rather odd.

"And she took pains to be as masculine as she could be. She dressed plainly, she used no colognes or toilet waters, she carried an electric shaver, though we must suppose it was never used. Because she couldn't grow an Adam's-apple she wore high necklines to cover her neck, and because she couldn't achieve on her forehead an M-line, she always wore a lock of hair falling over her brow."

"What d'you mean?" said Burden. "An M-line?"

"Look in the mirror," said Wexford.

The three men got up and confronted themselves in the ornamented glass on the wall above their table. "See," said Wexford, putting his own hands up to his scanty hairline, and the other two perceived how their hair receded in two triangles at the temples. "All men," he said, "have that in some degree, but no woman does. Her hairline is oval in shape. But for Rhoda Comfrey these were small matters and easily dealt with. It was only when she paid a rare visit to Kingsmarkham to see her father that she was obliged to go back to being a woman. Oh, and on one other occasion. No wonder people said she was happy in London and miserable in the country. For her, dressing as a woman was very much what it would be like for a normal man to be forced into drag.

"But she played it in character, or in her old character, dressing fussily, wearing heavy make-up, painting her fingernails which, however, she couldn't grow long for the purpose. For these visits she kept women's underclothes and an old pair of stiletto-heeled shoes. When you come to think of it, she might buy a woman's dress without trying it on, but hardly a pair of shoes."

"But you said," put in Griswold, "that there were other occasions when she went back to being a woman."

"I said there was one, sir. She might deceive her friends and her acquaintances. They weren't going to subject her to a physical examination. She had been a patient of old Dr. Castle in Kingsmarkham, though I imagine she was a strong healthy woman who seldom needed medical attention. Last year, however, he died, but when she suspected she had appendicitis, she had to go to a doctor. Even the most cursory examination would have revealed she was no man, so to Dr. Lomond she went reluctantly as a woman, giving her true name and an address she thought up on the way. Hence, the Farriner confusion.

"That was a year ago, by which time she had already met Polly Flinders—and Polly Flinders had fallen in love with her."

23

"Everything points to Rhoda Comfrey's having been aware of the girl's feelings," Wexford went on, "and to some extent to her having encouraged them. She let her act as her secretary instead of just an occasional typist, took her into the wine bar for drinks, drove her home if she was kept late at Elm Green, sent her whimsical postcards. What she did not do, and prob-

ably felt she was behaving ethically in not doing—
although I dare say she didn't want to either—was
show her the least demonstrative affection."

"It was cruel and unjustifiable all the same," said
Burden.

"I think it was natural," Wexford said hesitantly.
"I think it was very *human*. After all, look at it from
Rhoda's point of view. As a girl of twenty-five she
hadn't been remotely attractive to men. Mustn't it have
enormously gratified her to know that at fifty she had
someone of twenty-five in love with her? A poor obtuse
innocent creature perhaps, but still a young human
being in love with her. A poor ill-favoured thing, but
mine own. Who else had ever really loved her? Her
mother, long ago. Mrs. Parker? This was a love of a
different kind, and the kind everyone wants once in a
lifetime."

Griswold had started to look impatient. "All right,
Reg, all right. Get back to the nitty-gritty, can't you?
You're a policeman, not a shrink."

"Well, for the nitty-gritty, sir, we have to come to a
month or so ago. Rhoda was planning to go on holiday,
but her father had had a stroke. She meant to go, no
doubt about that, but perhaps she ought to see the old
man first and find out how the land lay."

"What d'you mean by that?"

"I mean that if he was very seriously incapacitated
she would know that her greatest fear, that her father
might have to be parked on her one day, would be
groundless and she could go off to France with a
light heart. But she had to go down there and find out,
even though this would mean putting off her holiday
for a day or two. Never mind. That was no great
inconvenience. She phoned her aunt to tell her she
would be coming, and when she did so Polly Flinders
was in the flat, but not all the time in the room.

"Now, if no one else did, Polly knew that Grenville
West had once or twice before disappeared mysteriously
at weekends. I think we can assume that Rhoda rather

enjoyed keeping her in the dark about that, and guessed she was giving her cause for jealousy. On that Friday evening Polly had very likely been trouble-some—she may, for instance have wanted West to take her away on holiday with him—and Rhoda vented her annoyance by calling Lilian Crown 'darling.' Polly overheard, as she was meant to overhear, and believed that West was involved with another woman living in the country. No doubt she asked questions, but was told it was no business of hers, so she determined to go to Stowerton on the Monday and find out for herself what was going on."

Burden interrupted him. "Why didn't Rhoda or West or whatever we're going to call him or her— it gets a bit complicated—go to Kingsmarkham that day? Then there wouldn't have been any need to postpone the holiday. Where does the Trieste Hotel come in?"

"Think about it," said Wexford. "Walk out of Elm Green in make-up and high-heeled shoes and a dress?"

"I should have thought a public lavatory . . ." Burden stopped himself proceeding further with this gaffe, but not in time to prevent Griswold's hoot of laughter.

"How does he manage to go in the Gents and come out of the Ladies, Mike?"

Wexford didn't feel like laughing. He had never been amused by drag or the idea of it, and now the humourous aspects of this particular case of cross-dressing seemed to him quenched by its consequences. "She used hotels for the change-over," he said rather coldly, "and usually hotels in some distant part of London. But this time she had left it too late to pick and choose, especially with the tourist season at its height. On that Saturday she must have tried to book in at a number of hotels without success. The only one which could take her was the Trieste which she had used once before—on the occasion of the visit to Dr. Lomond. You can see, Mike, how she walked out of the Trieste on that day, crossed Montfort Circus, went up Montfort Hill, and chose an address from a street name and an advertisement.

"So back to the Trieste she went, with her car packed up for the French holiday and allowing Vivian to believe she was leaving directly for France. The car was left in a garage at the hotel with her passport and French currency locked up in the boot. On her person she retained the car keys and her new wallet, and these went into her handbag when on the following day she left the hotel as Rhoda Comfrey."

"That must have been as bad as walking out of Elm Green. Suppose she'd been seen?"

"By whom? A hotel servant? She says she's calling on her friend, Mr. West. It would have been easy enough to mingle with the other guests or conceal herself in a cloakroom, say, if Hetherington had appeared. As a respectable middle-aged lady, she'd hardly have been suspected of being there for what you'd call an immoral purpose."

"Hotels don't take much notice of that these days," said the Chief Constable easily. Forgetting perhaps that it was he who had told Wexford to get back to the nitty-gritty, he said, "This passport, though. I'm still not clear about it. I see she had to have a man's name and a man's identity, but why that one? She could have changed her name by deed poll or kept Comfrey and used one of those Christian names that will do for either sex. Leslie, for instance, or Cecil."

"Deed poll means a certain amount of publicity, sir. But I don't think that was entirely the reason. She needed a passport. Of course she could have used some ambiguous Christian name for that. And with her birth certificate and her change-of-name document she could have submitted to the Passport Office a photograph that gave no particular indication of whether she was male or female . . ."

"Exactly," said Griswold. "A British passport isn't

required to state the holder's home address or marital status or," he added with some triumph, "the holder's sex."

"No, sir, not in so many words. If the holder is accompanied by a child, that child must be declared as male or female, but not the holder. Yet on the cover and on page one the holder's *style* is shown. It wouldn't have helped her much, would it, to have a man's Christian name and a man's photograph but be described as *Miss* Cecil Comfrey?"

"You're a shrewd man, Reg," said the Chief Constable.

Wexford said laconically, "Thanks," and remembered that it wasn't long since that same voice had called him a foolish one. "Instead she chose to acquire and submit the birth certificate of a man who would never need a passport because he would never, in any conceivable circumstances, be able to leave this country. She chose to assume the identity of her mentally defective and crippled first cousin. And to him, I discovered yesterday, she left everything she possessed when she died and her royalties as long as they continue."

"They won't do poor John West much good," said Burden. "What happened when Polly encountered Rhoda on the Monday evening?"

Not much caring what reaction he would get, Wexford said, "At the beginning of *Apes in Hell,* two lines are quoted from Beaumont and Fletcher's play:

" 'Those have most power to hurt us, that we love;
  We lay our sleeping lives within their arms.'

"Rhoda wrote that book long before she met Polly. I wonder if she ever thought what they really meant or ever thought about them again. Possibly she did. Possibly she understood that Polly had laid her sleeping life within her arms, and that though she might have to repudiate the girl, she must never let her know the true state of affairs. For eonists, Ellis tells us, are often 'educated, sensitive, refined and reserved.'

"On that Monday evening Polly came to the gates of Stowerton Infirmary prepared to see something which would make her upset and unhappy. She expected to see West either with another woman or on his way to see another woman. At first she didn't see West at all. She joined the bus queue, watching a much bedizened middle-aged woman who was in conversation with an old woman. When did she realise? I don't know. It may be that at first she took Rhoda for some relative of West's, even perhaps a sister. But one of the things we can never disguise is the way we walk. Rhoda never attempted to disguise her voice. Polly got on the bus and went upstairs, feeling that the unbelievable was happening. But she followed Rhoda and they met on that footpath.

"What she saw when they confronted each other must have been enough to cause a temporary loss of reason. Remember, she had come, prepared to be distressed, but nothing had prepared her for this. Marie Cole's shock would have been nothing to hers. She saw, in fact, a travesty in the true meaning of the word, and she stabbed to death an abomination."

Griswold looked embarrassed. "Pity she couldn't have seen it for what it was, a lucky escape for her."

"I think she saw it as the end of the world," Wexford said sombrely. "It was only later on that she came to feel anything would be preferable to having it known she'd been in love with a man who was no man at all. And that's why she agreed to my story."

"Cheer up, Reg," said the Chief Constable. "We're used to you breaking the rules. You always do." He laughed, adding, "The end justifies the means," as if this aphorism were invariably accepted by all as pithy truth instead of having for centuries occasioned controversy. "Let's all have another drink before they shut up shop."

"Not for me, sir," said Wexford. "Good night." And he walked out into the dark and went home, leaving his superior planning reprisals and his subordinate affectionately incensed.

ABOUT THE AUTHOR

RUTH RENDELL is the author of fourteen previous mystery novels, including *The Face of Trespass, Some Lie and Some Die, Murder Being Once Done, Shake Hands Forever, No More Dying Then* and *One Across, Two Down.* Her latest novel, *A Demon in My View*, was awarded the 1976 Golden Dagger Award by the British Crime Writers Association. In July 1986, Bantam will publish *A Dark-Adapted Eye*, written by Ruth Rendell under the pseudonym of Barbara Vine. A former journalist, she lives with her husband and son outside of London.

Dear Reader,

There is nothing unusual in having two Christian names, but perhaps it is less common to be called by each of them equally. This is what happened to me. Ruth was my father's choice of name for me, Barbara my mother's. Because Ruth was difficult for my mother's Scandinavian parents to pronounce, her side of the family called me Barbara, and since this sort of duality was impossible in one household, my father finally started calling me Barbara too.

I tend to divide friends and relatives into the "Ruth people" and the "Barbara people." Both names are equally familiar to me, equally "my" names. If either were called out in the street I would turn around. And I don't mind which I am called so long as people don't try to change in, so to speak, midstream. There is for me something grotesque in a Barbara person trying to become a Ruth person, or vice-versa. Only my husband knows as well as I do into which category each friend falls. He can write the Christmas cards and always get them right. But he never calls me by either of my Christian names.

It has always interested me—I don't think my parents realized this—that both my names mean or imply "a stranger in a strange land," Ruth who was exiled into an alien country, Barbara that signifies "a foreigner."

Growing up with two names doesn't make you into two people. It does give you two aspects of personality, and Ruth and Barbara are two aspects of me. Ruth is tougher, colder, more analytical, possibly more aggressive. Ruth has written all the novels, created Chief Inspector Wexford. Ruth is the professional writer. Barbara is more feminine. It is Barbara who sews. If Barbara writes it is letters that she writes.

For a long time I have wanted Barbara to have a voice as well as Ruth. It would be a softer voice speaking at a slower pace, more sensitive perhaps, and more intuitive. In A DARK-ADAPTED EYE she has found that voice, taking a surname from the other side of the family, the paternal side, for Vine was my great-grandmother's maiden name. There would be nothing surprising to a psychologist in Barbara's choosing, as she asserts herself, to address readers in the first person.

The novel itself is the story of Faith Severn, and her exploration of circumstances that led to a terrible murder in her family more than thirty years before. I hope you will enjoy reading this book, as much as Barbara Vine enjoyed writing it.

Sincerely,

Ruth Rendell

1

On the morning Vera died I woke up very early. The birds had started, more of them and singing more loudly in our leafy suburb than in the country. They never sang like that outside Vera's windows in the Vale of Dedham. I lay there listening to something repeating itself monotonously. A thrush, it must have been, doing what Browning said it did and singing each song twice over. It was a Thursday in August, a hundred years ago. Not much more than a third of that, of course. It only feels so long.

In these circumstances alone one knows when someone is going to die. All other deaths can be predicted, conjectured, even anticipated with some certainty, but not to the hour, the minute, with no room for hope. Vera would die at eight o'clock and that was that. I began to feel sick. I lay there exaggeratedly still, listening for some sound from the next room. If I was awake my father would be. About my mother

I was less sure. She had never made a secret of her dislike of both his sisters. It was one of the things which had made a rift between them, though there they were together in the next room, in the same bed still. People did not break a marriage, leave each other, so lightly in those days.

I thought of getting up but first I wanted to make sure where my father was. There was something terrible in the idea of encountering him in the passage, both of us dressing-gowned, thick-eyed with sleeplessness, each seeking the bathroom and each politely giving way to the other. Before I saw him I needed to be washed and brushed and dressed, my loins girded. I could hear nothing but that thrush uttering its idiot phrase five or six times over, not twice.

To work he would go as usual, I was sure of that. And Vera's name would not be mentioned. None of it had been spoken about at all in our house since the last time my father went to see Vera. There was one crumb of comfort for him. No one knew. A man may be very close to his sister, his twin, without anyone knowing of the relationship, and none of our neighbours knew he was Vera Hillyard's brother. None of the bank's clients knew. If today the head cashier remarked upon Vera's death, as he very likely might, as people would by reason of her sex among other things, I knew my father would present to him a bland, mildly interested face and utter some suitable · platitude. He had, after all, to survive.

A floorboard creaked in the passage. I heard the bedroom door close and then the door of the bathroom, so I got up and looked at the day. A clean white still morning, with no sun and no blue in the sky, a morning that seemed to me to be waiting because I was. Six-thirty. There was an angle you could stand at looking out of this window where you could see no other house, so plentiful were the trees and shrubs, so thick their foliage. It was like looking into a clearing in a rather elaborate wood. Vera used to sneer at where my parents lived, saying it was neither town nor country.

My mother was up now. We were all stupidly early, as if we were going away on holiday. When I used to go to Sindon I was sometimes up as early as this, excited and looking forward to it. How could I have looked forward to the society of Vera, an unreasonable carping scold when on her own with me. and, when Eden was there, the two of them closing ranks to exclude anyone who might try to penetrate their alliance? I hoped, I suppose. Each time I was older and because of this she might change. She never did—until almost the end. And by then she was too desperate for an ally to be choosy.

I went to the bathroom. It was always possible to tell if my father had finished in the bathroom. He used an old-fashioned cut-throat razor and wiped the blade after each stroke on a small square of newspaper. The newspaper and the jug of hot water he fetched himself but the remains were always left for my mother to clear away, the square of paper with its load of shaving soap full of stubble, the empty jug. I washed in cold water. In summer, we only lit the boiler once a week for baths. Vera and Eden bathed every day, and that was one of the things I *had* liked about Sindon, my daily bath, though Vera's attitude always was that I would have escaped it if I could.

The paper had come. It was tomorrow the announcement would be, of course, a few bald lines. Today there was nothing about Vera. She was stale, forgotten, until this morning when, in a brief flare-up, the whole country would talk of her, those who deplored and those who said it served her right. My father sat at the dining-table, reading the paper. It was the *Daily Telegraph*, than which no other daily paper was ever read in our family. The crossword puzzle he would save for the evening, just as Vera had done, once only in all the years phoning my father for the solution to a clue that was driving her crazy. When Eden had a home of her own and was rich, she often rang him up and got him to finish the puzzle for her over the phone. She had never been as good at it as they.

He looked up and nodded to me. He didn't

smile. The table had yesterday's cloth on it, yellow check not to show the egg stains. Food was still rationed, meat being very scarce, and we ate eggs all the time, laid by my mother's chickens. Hence the crowing cockerels in our garden suburb, the fowl runs concealed behind hedges of lonicera and laurel. We had no eggs that morning, though. No cornflakes either. My mother would have considered cornflakes frivolous, in their white and orange packet. She had disliked Vera, had no patience with my father's intense family love, but she had a strong sense of occasion, of what was fitting. Without a word, she brought us toast that, while hot, had been thinly spread with margarine, a jar of marrow and ginger jam, a pot of tea.

I knew I shouldn't be able to eat. He ate. Business was to be as usual with him, I could tell that. It was over, wiped away, a monstrous effort made, if not to forget, at least to behave as if all was forgotten. The silence was broken by his voice, harsh and stagy, reading aloud. It was something about the war in Korea. He read on and on, columns of it, and it became embarrassing to listen because no one reads like that without introduction, explanation, excuse. It must have gone on for ten minutes. He read to the foot of the page, to where presumably you were told the story was continued inside. He didn't turn over. He broke off in mid-sentence. 'In the Far,' he said, never getting to 'East' but laying the paper down, aligning the pages, folding it twice, and once more, so that it was back in the shape it had been when the boy pushed it through the letterbox.

'In the far' hung in the air, taking on a curious significance, quite different from what the writer had intended. He took another piece of toast but got no further towards eating it. My mother watched him. I think she had been tender with him once but he had had no time for it or room for it and so her tenderness had withered for want of encouragement. I did not expect her to go to him and take his hand or put her arms round him. Would I have done so myself if she had not been there? Perhaps. That family's mutual love had not usually found its expression in outward show. In other words, there had not been embraces. The twins, for instance, did not kiss each other, though the women pecked the air around each other's faces.

It was a quarter to eight now. I kept repeating over and over to myself (like the thrush, now silent), 'In the far, in the far'. When first it happened, when he was told, he went into paroxysms of rage, of disbelief, of impotent protest.

'Murdered, murdered!' he kept shouting, like someone in an Elizabethan tragedy, like someone who bursts into a castle hall with dreadful news. And then, 'My sister!' and 'My poor sister!' and 'My little sister!'

But silence and concealment fell like a shutter. It was lifted briefly, after Vera was dead, when, sitting in a closed room after dark, like conspirators, he and I heard from Josie what happened that April day. He never spoke of it again. His twin was erased from his mind and he even made himself—incredibly—into an only child. Once I heard him tell someone that he had never regretted having no brothers or sisters.

It was only when he was ill and not far from death himself that he resurrected memories of his sisters. And the stroke he had had, as if by some physiological action stripping away layers of reserve and inhibition, making him laugh sometimes and just as often cry, released an unrestrained gabbling about how he had felt that summer. His former love for Vera the repressive years had turned to repulsion and fear, his illusions broken as much by the tug-of-war and Eden's immorality—his word, not mine—as by the murder itself. My mother might have said, though she did not, that at last he was seeing his sisters as they really were.

He left the table, his tea half-drunk, his second piece of toast lying squarely in the middle of his plate, the *Telegraph* folded and lying with its edges compulsively lined up to the table corner. No word was spoken to my mother and me. He went upstairs, he came down, the front door closed behind him. He would walk the leafy roads, I thought, making detours, turning the half mile to the station into two miles, hiding from the time in places where there were no clocks. It was then that I noticed he had left his watch on the table. I picked up the paper and there was the watch underneath.

'We should have gone away somewhere,' I said.

My mother said fiercely, 'Why should we? She hardly ever came here. Why should we let her drive us away?'

'Well, we haven't,' I said.

I wondered which was right, the clock on the wall that said five to eight or my father's watch that said three minutes to. My own watch was upstairs. Time passes so slowly over such points in it. There still seemed an aeon to wait. My mother loaded the tray and took it into the kitchen, making a noise about it, banging cups, a way of showing that it was no fault of hers. Innocent herself, she had been dragged into this family by marriage, all unknowing. It was another matter for me who was of their blood.

I went upstairs. My watch was in the bed-side table. It was new, a present bestowed by my parents for getting my degree. That, because of what had happened, it was a less good degree than everyone had expected, no one had commented upon. The watch face was small, not much larger than the cluster of little diamonds in my engagement ring that lay beside it, and you had to get close up to it to read the hands. I thought, in a moment the heavens will fall, there will be a great bolt of thunder, nature could not simply ignore. There was nothing. Only the birds had become silent, which they would do anyway at this time, their territorial claims being made, their trees settled on, the business of their day begun. What would the business of my day be? One thing I thought I would do. I would phone Helen, I would talk to Helen. Symbolic of my attitude to my engagement, my future marriage, this was, that it was to Helen I meant to fly for comfort, not the man who had given me the ring with a diamond cluster as big as a watch face.

I walked over to the bedside table, stagily, self-consciously, like a bad actress in an amateur production. The director would have halted me and told me to do it again, to walk away and do it again. I nearly did walk away so as not to see the time. But I picked up the watch and looked and had a long, rolling, falling feeling through my body as I saw that I had missed the moment. It was all over now and she was dead. The hands of the watch stood at five past eight.

The only kind of death that can be accurately predicted to the minute had taken place, the death that takes its victim,

> . . . feet foremost through the floor,
> Into an empty space.

Special Offer
Buy a Bantam Book
for only 50¢.

Now you can have an up-to-date listing of Bantam's hundreds of titles plus take advantage of our unique and exciting bonus book offer. A special offer which gives you the opportunity to purchase a Bantam book for only 50¢. Here's how!

By ordering any five books at the regular price per order, you can also choose any other single book listed (up to a $4.95 value) for just 50¢. Some restrictions do apply, but for further details why not send for Bantam's listing of titles today!

Just send us your name and address and we will send you a catalog!

Murder, that most foul of crimes, appears to be the most _British of crimes_ in the hands of these two Bantam authors:

From Patricia Wentworth:

Maud Silver, Private Enquiry Agent, is everybody's favorite spinster-detective. From her Edwardian hairstyle to her beaded shoes, she is the very model of a governess, her occupation before she decided to take on the more challenging occupation of a private enquiry agent. Armed with stubborn British common sense and an iron will to succeed, she is one of the best at tracking murder . . . and so will you be as you follow close behind her on the trail of clues in each of these Patricia Wentworth mysteries from Bantam:

From Catherine Aird:

The charm and wit that have made Aird's Detective Inspector C. D. Sloan a classic among British Sleuths will draw you into the tangled webs of clues, misdeeds and intrigues that Sloan must unravel in each of these fine titles from Bantam:

Look for them at your bookstore or use this handy coupon: